SUICIDE LAKE

SUICIDE LAKE

SOMETIMES SMALL TOWNS ARE DANGEROUS PLACES

A ROMANTIC SUSPENSE NOVEL BY

ASHLEY FONTAINNE

Cover and Interior book design by One of a Kind
Covers

SUICIDE LAKE

or it was not purchased for your use only, then
please purchase your own copy. Thank you for
respecting the hard work of this author.

Published by RMSW Press, LLC

ISBN 13: 978-0692648926
ISBN 10: 0692648925

This book was produced using Pressbooks.com,
and PDF rendering was done by PrinceXML.

CONTENTS

Chapter One

THERE WAS NO movie magic to accompany my final act. No music building to a crescendo. No long-lost loved one rushing in breathlessly at the last moment to save me from my wretched plans. No adorable, furry creatures sneaking up from out of nowhere to rest a hairy head in my lap, eyes beseeching me to stop. No close up face shots of me sitting on the edge of the long deck at sunset while tears slowly streamed down my face. Because this was real life, not some scripted Hollywood blockbuster.

My final m oments w ere g reeted b y the gentle lapping of water at the edge of the bank and the distant chirping of birds streaking through the colorful sky. No more, no less.

My bare feet grazed the surface of the cold water. The cool, October air from two days ago had been replaced by a warm breeze. The Indian summer had released a horde of mosquitoes. They buzzed around my head while others converged into a thick cloud inches above the water's surface.

Bradford Lake used to be a popular spot for people to visit with their children, but now, its reputation was tainted and no one came to enjoy the secluded place. The lake was a natural one, however, it had been the dumping ground for chemicals and waste products from local sawmills and farms. By the time the EPA stepped in during the 1970s after numerous protests from concerned residents, it was too late. Access to the lake was closed the year I turned ten. The water was foul and full of all sorts of bacteria and garbage. After several people turned up sick from swimming or boating in the dirty water, people found other watering holes to play in.

The lake's reputation wasn't helped any from another problem. Multiple suicides throughout the years, committed by people jumping off of the edge of the dock, changed everyone's perception of the area.

Locals nicknamed the place Suicide Lake. Most of the residents of Whitten County feared the mountain lake was haunted from all the lonely souls who ended their time on earth with one jump.

My ex-mother-in-law mentioned numerous times how in her younger days, folks traveled for miles to catch a glimpse of the epic sunsets and play in the placid, blue water. Those silly conversations about trivial, bullshit-thoughts drove me crazy during the last two months. I considered them Eleanor Runsford's way of trying to make up for all the years she looked the other way while her son used me as his personal punching bag.

All of the jumpers were women, and all of them had a common thread: abusive husbands or boyfriends. When Eleanor broached the subject, she'd always tear up, mentioning how traumatized the poor women must have been to settle on suicide as the only way out. "There are ways, agencies in place to assist women in those types of situations, so why didn't they use them?" was one of Eleanor's go-to responses.

My answer was the same as well. "How do you know they didn't try? People tend to whitewash or overlook what goes on behind closed doors."

Eleanor never discussed the horrors her son inflicted on me. God, even after all these years, I still can't say his name out loud. She even stood by him after he was convicted and sent to prison for killing his second wife. Fifteen years was his punishment after a wicked brawl while in the midst of a drug-induced haze.

Fifteen years.
How was the sentence fair?
Just?

Righteous?

He'd beaten the woman to death with his bare hands after finding out she'd been unfaithful. The jury bought into the lies told by his attorney that the act wasn't premeditated and he'd been convicted of manslaughter rather than murder. A life was over in minutes after sustaining multiple blows to the head, abdomen, and chest, yet it wasn't murder. I found the whole mess preposterous. A woman's last moments on earth were full of terror and pain. And all the bastard got was fifteen years?

It wasn't justice.

Not even close.

The sick freak wouldn't spend the full fifteen behind bars. He'd get paroled after being "rehabilitated" and then be released back into society while his victim rotted in the grave. In fact, Eleanor left an open letter from the Arkansas State Parole Board on the table last week. I read it, and it turned my stomach. Next month the slime-ball was up for parole. Just the notion he might be released and move back to town made my head spin. More reasons—the unfairness of the world around me, and the terror of my ex coming back—were why I was ready to leave.

I shouldn't have thought about Eleanor. Stupid, blind, crazy old bat. The bitch's way of dealing with the nightmare the fruit of her loins beat into me was to bring up the demise of strangers. I would have preferred we talk about real, painful feelings from real, painful events, yet the discussions never happened.

Ever the doting mother, one unable to see the real face behind the mask of humanity her son wore, Eleanor refused to view her child as a killer. She blamed the "tragedy" on drugs.

Typical.

Looking up at the orange and pink rays from the setting sun, I grimaced at what a messed up life I'd lived. Some of the madness was my own fault—I wasn't afraid to shoulder a bit of the blame. The therapists I'd been forced to see a variety of times during my life assured me of that fact with damn near the exact same phrase: none of this was your fault, Renee.

Consoling words; mind numbing pills; an admission to the psych ward. From all of that, I came to the conclusion it didn't matter where the faults were placed.

What mattered was simple: I lived with them and now I wouldn't.

POOR ME.

Poor little Renee Michelle Runsford, *nee*, Thornton.

That's what people would say when my body was discovered, all bloated and flesh missing from being nibbled on by fish. Yet another sad story to be passed around on social media then forgotten. Boom! A big firework exploding in the sky for all to see and ogle. A burst of excitement for people to *ooohh* and *aaahh* over. When the bright lights disappeared, memories of me would last no longer than the smoky remnants.

Boo-freaking-hoo.

I threw a pebble into the water, watching the ripples spread out from the point of entry. They started out small then widened into large, lopsided circles. Some of the edges caught the orange rays of the disappearing sun, making the water look like it was on fire.

I didn't miss the comparison to my life.

THE FIRST BIG boulder that crashed into my personal space happened at thirteen. Up until then, though not anywhere near close to the words *normal* or *perfect*, my life had been...tolerable. My father, the late, great piece of shit known to others as Raymond Thornton, disappeared from my life. Mom—the always sad and perpetually whiny Caroline Clark Thornton, told me dear old Dad found a new family to spend time with rather than us.

I was so hurt, so saddened to see Mom in such pain, I didn't question her story. I was too preoccupied with other things like helping to pay the bills and attempting to maintain my grades. Determined to be supportive, I lied about my age and snagged my first job at a laundromat. The pay was pathetic yet it did help put food on the table.

Unfortunately, some of the money made its way to Gene's Liquor Store and bought bottles of wine. I didn't realize the connection until a few years later. By then, it was too late to help. Caroline Thornton was a raging alcoholic.

THE NEXT ROCK thrown into my personal pond happened three years later and I still felt the ripples even after all this time. After a long Saturday working at the laundromat, I arrived home and discovered Mom in a drunken stupor. Unlike most times when she overindulged and simply cried herself to sleep, ol' Caroline Thornton was on a rampage. The ugly memories clouded my vision, my mother's words as fresh in my mind as the day she spoke them.

"He left us! The no good, dirty, piece-of-shit! Left us to fend for ourselves. How could he? I mean, he married *the* Caroline Clark! I was homecoming queen, you know. Could've had any man I wanted in this county, but I picked him. Gave him a family. Took care of our home. Cooked dinner. *Serviced* him whenever he wanted. Ungrateful bastard."

"Mom, I think you've had enough for one night."

"Don't you talk to me like I'm a child, Renee! I'm the mother here. I'll say when I've had enough, and I haven't yet. Don't think there's enough booze in the world to forget what he did to me. To us."

"Okay, Mom. I'm going to fix some coffee. It's been a really long day. Would you like some?"

"Oh, my sweet Renee. Always looking out for me. Of course I would. You make the best coffee."

"Thanks. I've had a lot of practice," I muttered.

Fortunately, Mom was too intoxicated to catch my heavy sarcasm.

"You should let me highlight your hair. It's too boring. You'll never catch a man with that pile of mouse fur on your head. Some blonde streaks would help. And why aren't you wearing any makeup? A lady should always put her best face on when she leaves the house. If you keep going out looking so frumpy, people will think you're nothing but poor, white trash. You could be beautiful, Renee, just like me, if you try a little."

"We are poor, Mom."

"Well, that certainly isn't my fault! It's your father's. I've been trying to get a raise at work, but so far, no luck."

"Maybe you should look for a different job, Mom. You've been slaving away at the store for years. If that doesn't work, Mr. Richardson might give you one if you quit missing so much work."

"Oh, little miss high and mighty! Big words coming from a girl who works in a

11

laundromat all day! What you do isn't *near* the stress I have at work. Period."

"Here, Mom. Have some hot coffee."

For a few minutes, the conversation dwindled down to nothing but sporadic comments about mundane things, mostly about my boring face, bland choice of clothing, and mousey hair. I thought the night would end on a somewhat normal note. I was used to Mom's constant bitching about my appearance.

Boy, was I wrong.

After Mom finished her coffee, she pushed the empty cup to the center of the table. She fumbled around looking for a cigarette in the pockets of her tattered robe. Twice, she nearly fell off the chair. Once she found the pack, lit one, blew a heavy plume of smoke from thin lips smeared with red lipstick, she dropped the bombshell.

"Your dad didn't leave us."

Stunned, I replied, "What do you mean? Yes he did! For that Cyndi chick who worked at Snack-n-Go. Remember?"

"I sort of lied. To protect you."

"Sort of lied to protect me? Exactly what does that mean? Did he leave you for another man or something?" I blurted out.

For the first time in years, Mom laughed. It was a strange sound, mixed with the heavy wetness constantly in the chest of a smoker. "Wow, sixteen and already a hard-core cynic. No, Renee, your dad wasn't gay. He was a cheater like I said. And he did have an affair with Cyndi Robertson."

Confused yet curious, I asked, "Then what part of your story was a lie?"

"That he left us."

Irritated at her drunken ramblings, I stood and went to the sink, unwilling to listen to any more of her words. "I'm going to take a shower and do my homework. Goodnight, Mom."

"No, you aren't. Sit down, I'm not finished with getting this off my chest. I've got to. If I don't, I think I'll go insane."

Mom never shared her innermost thoughts and feelings with me. Something about the tone of her voice made the hairs stand up on my arms. "I'm listening."

"I suspected he was cheating, so one night, I followed him. He said he was going for a ride on his Harley to clear his head. I knew he was lying because I saw it behind his eyes. Sure enough, I caught them together at Bradford Lake. Oh, I was so angry. One minute, I was screaming and yelling at them both, and the next, I was standing at the water's edge covered in blood."

"You...are you saying you killed Dad?" I whispered.

"Yep. And Cyndi. Took a tire iron and smashed their cheating heads in. Dumped them and the bike in the lake and came home."

MOM'S WORDS HAD burned a hole in my chest. I left that night, running out of the house despite her drunken pleas to come back. I ran down the dark street of our trailer park, through the center of town, out past the baseball fields, until I collapsed into a sobbing heap.

The only comfort I found was in the arms of the man who would end up being my ex. He happened by and saw me crying and pulled up. His strong arms enveloped me in a warm embrace while I wept. He didn't ask what was wrong, just provided companionship.

Oh, and a bottle of tequila, which we drank together under the moonlight until both of us were so drunk, I'm not sure how we ended up having sex.

We did, and the stick turned blue two months later.

A month before I gave birth, Mom died in a car accident on her way home from a bar, and I married the father of my child. A sweet, baby boy we named William who only lived for six months. Burying the little body of my son sent me on a trip inside a psychiatric hospital.

Things had been screwed up ever since.

Now I was homeless after losing my oh-so-exciting menial job. The job prospects were nil for a forty-nine-year-old high school dropout living in a small town. With minimal education, I didn't qualify for much. I couldn't compete with young, twenty-somethings who were well schooled in technology. Unemployment kept me fed and the lights on but wasn't enough to pay the mortgage. After six months, the minuscule checks stopped. I couldn't even afford the filing fee for bankruptcy.

No siblings. No children. No extended family. No close friends willing to take me in, so things boiled down to one, horrifying truth.

I'd been forced to rely on a woman who for years had been a painful thorn in my side. With my house in foreclosure, I swallowed my pride and showed up on the doorstep of Eleanor Runsford. To her credit, she opened the door and ushered me inside. I'd been living in a back bedroom, hiding from the world, for two months.

God really had a sick sense of humor and to be quite honest, I was tired of it.

Staring down at the worn out comforter

I brought with me, I let a deep sigh escape, feeling oddly connected to the disheveled rag. At one point, it had been a vibrant collage of colors, loved by someone, a warm treasure they snuggled up to every night.

Not anymore. The colors had faded into a dingy mishmash of nothing, a used up rag cared for by no one. Tossed uncaringly into a back bedroom where no one would see it. Just like me. No one would ever miss the pile of material should it disappear, and I doubted anyone would really miss me, either.

I ROLLED THE full bottle of Xanax around in my hands for the longest moment. The small piece of plastic, a worthless outer shell that would serve as proof I took my own life, was one of the last things I would ever touch.

How utterly symbolic.

Although Eleanor had a myriad of medications to choose from, Xanax seemed the fastest avenue and was the one she had the most of. This was not the first t ime I contemplated killing myself but I had never come this close to actually accomplishing it. The previous times I entertained these thoughts I was like Hamlet, lamenting my lot in life and all the sadness and pain that had been my constant companion. All the other times I stopped myself, unwilling to end my life for fear of God's retribution against suicide.

When these morbid, suicidal thoughts entered my mind, it was due to a panicked state I created over an event leading me to want to end it all. I would bounce between hysterical crying jags to under-the-covers-for-days bouts of depression.

This time was different. My mind was no longer like a ball bouncing around a tennis court. No more thoughts bounding wildly from one side to the other. A few weeks ago, I began wandering into the deepest, darkest recesses and crouched in the back corner, closing every tie to my world as I went. And as my mind retreated, my soul followed, veering so far away from God I just didn't care anymore if offing myself would damn me for all eternity.

Hell, I was damned right here on Earth already.

Fear of fire and brimstone was replaced by this constant throbbing of mind-numbing memories. My new medical issues didn't help any, either. I wanted more than anything to vanquish everything away. To blink my eyes just once and start over; to be the recipient of some other-worldly miracle. Seriously, just to clasp, even if only briefly, onto the notion that there was some sort of hope.

Those wishes never came to pass, so here I sat, ready for the end.

The enjoyment of life had been drained from my body and soul with each wound I sustained over the years. I was being bled dry and the final mortal wounds came this year, one right after another. Vicious blows that didn't just knock me on my ass but stomped me into the ground. Now, I was a lifeless corpse stumbling through life with no purpose or direction.

It was time to go. Time to join the others and take the plunge into Suicide Lake.

I LOOKED OUT across the water and over to the tree line. Gray, leafless and dead; a perfect summation of what my life had become. My final day in this wretched world and my last view was of dead trees, a used up comforter, and gripping a plastic pill bottle.

Why would I have expected more?

Uncapping the lid, I shook out my salvation, counting them as I went. Twenty pills seemed enough to do the trick, so I grabbed my water bottle in my lap to chase the first three down, putting the remainder back in the bottle. I wanted my body to become as tranquil as the water in front of me, ready for the constant ache in my back and heart, to cease.

The sun was almost gone. Three pills downed, I stopped. Before swallowing another, I took in one last look of the beautiful lake. I understood, fully and completely, why others came to this spot to end their lives. The tranquility was a welcome reprieve from the chaotic world. A final memory burned into the brain of peace and beauty.

I glanced back down when something hard bumped against my foot. The last glint of the sun's rays danced on the top of the water. Squinting, I noticed the dark, red glow was back.

Instead of basking in the lovely color on the gentle ripples, I screamed.

The red sheen wasn't from the sun.

It was from blood, and it coated my feet, which rested right next to a stiff hand poking up from the depths below.

I jumped to my feet, scrambling to get away from the corpse. The comforter, water bottle, and pills went flying. Instead of going after them, I let them disappear under the water.

Heart pounding and body shaking, I backed away from the edge of the boardwalk.

My first instinct was to grab my cell and call for help. I felt around in my pocket, only to remember I didn't bring it with me because it had been turned off three days earlier for nonpayment.

"Damnit!"

"Ma'am? Are you okay?"

Spinning around, I came face-to-face with a man. It took me several seconds to realize he was a cop.

And I knew him.

"Clifton! You scared the shit out of me! What are you...oh, never mind. I'm just glad you're here. I, uh, didn't bring my phone, so I was going to head to town and call for help."

Clifton Simpson walked toward me. In the dimming light, dressed in his uniform with the vest underneath giving him extra padding, he seemed bigger than I remembered.

"Renee? Renee Runsford?"

"Thornton. I changed back after my divorce."

Clifton moved closer, all of his six-foot-plus frame only inches away. He smelled like stale coffee, sweat, and cheap cologne. I hadn't seen him in years but recognized the thick head of jet black hair—now interspersed with flecks of white—and his deep, rhythmic voice. How I didn't hear him walking down the boardwalk earlier escaped me. Guess I was too wrapped up with thoughts of my horrible life.

"Oh, that's right. Forgot. Sorry. So, we got a call from a concerned citizen. Said they saw a woman sitting out here on the edge of the dock, alone. Asked for a unit to stop by and check it out, so here I am. What are you doing out here, Renee? You been drinking? You look unsteady."

"My mother was the drinker in my family, not me, so no. I look unsteady because I just touched a dead body."

"Excuse me?" Clifton replied. His forehead knitted together in disbelief and confusion. "A body?"

Stepping away, I moved to the edge of the dock and pointed. "Yeah, body. Didn't you hear me scream?"

Clifton pulled out a flashlight and

walked past me, peering over the edge. "I did, but thought...oh, shit. Doesn't really matter at this point what I thought."

Backing away, Clifton put his arm on my chest, forcing me to step back. He grabbed the microphone on his shoulder and radioed for assistance.

The warm breeze from earlier was gone, along with the annoying mosquitoes. Darkness settled like a death shroud over the lake. A chill of fear made me shiver. Clifton noticed and led me to his unit. He pulled out a jacket and handed it to me.

"You should've worn something warmer," he said.

"Wasn't planning on staying out here long," I grumbled. My mood was deteriorating as the Xanax flowed through my veins. Sirens wailed in the distance. "May I go now? Sounds like your buddies are close."

"Sorry, Renee, but you'll need to stay here until one of the detectives speak with you."

Aghast, worried they'd notice I was

barred out, I opened my mouth to protest. I shut it just as fast when I remembered the pills—and the bottle with Eleanor's name—had fallen into the lake.

The radio on Clifton's shoulder crackled to life, saving me from having to respond. The sirens were closer and I could see headlights bouncing through the winding road leading to the lake.

So much for a quiet, peaceful evening to end my life. There certainly would be noise and activity now.

Damn.

Of course, someone else's tragedy trumped my own.

Figures.

Chapter Two

THE BIG, MOUNTAIN of a man leaned
against the hood of Clifton's unit. His eyes
were dark brown and full of accusations
swimming around in the murkiness. He was
busy staring at the others processing the
scene, Eleanor's pill bottle in his hand. At
only five-foot-three, I felt like a dwarf
standing next to him. Detective Richard
Greenwood had to be at least six-two. Since
he'd acted like one from the moment he

pounced on me, I mentally nicknamed him Detective Dick.

"Tell me again why you came out here?" he asked.

He was chewing on a straw like it was his lover's ear. The disgusting sounds and wiggles from the piece of plastic reminded me of the times my mother tried to quit smoking. Perhaps he was, too, and maybe lack of nicotine soured his normally peppy demeanor.

I withheld a chuckle at the thought. There was no way, not even when a baby, Detective Dick had been peppy. Or happy. He wore edginess and anger like accessories to compliment the worn-out dress shirt, khaki pants, and days' worth of stubble. He could step onto the set of any cop show and fit right in.

The noise level around the boardwalk was ridiculous. It looked like the entire group of emergency personnel of Whitten County came out to investigate. Blue lights from patrol cars filled t he d ark area, competing for attention with the flashing red ones off the ambulance. Shaking my head, I wondered why an ambulance had been dispatched. The body was dead, so why not just send the meat wagon from the coroner's office?

"Mrs. Runsford, did you hear me?"

"Uh, as I mentioned twice, my name's Ms. Thornton. Yes, I heard you. I'm cold and tired of yelling over all this noise. Oh, and freaked out. I've already gone over this twice. Can't I just go home? I told you what little I know."

"Deputy Simpson must have given me the wrong name. Sorry about that," he replied, scribbling notes on a pad. "Would you prefer to go over your statement again at the station?"

I didn't like the tone in his voice—or the bald-faced lie. He'd worked the homicide investigation when my ex killed his wife. We'd only met in person once after he came by to question me about my experiences with my batterer. He was ugly and rude back then, too. When I wouldn't offer up anything to help him, he'd flown into a rage. The way

I figured i t, n o o ne h elped m e w hen I filed reports of abuse. My words didn't mean anything back then, so why would they hold more weight because the bastard finally did to someone else what he tried to do to me for years?

The accusatory eyes glared at me, and a hint of irritation seeped into Detective Dick's voice. Anger bubbled inside my chest, which was sort of nice. It helped warm me up. "No. I'd prefer to go home and take a hot shower. I still have blood on my feet. That's just plain unsanitary."

"Looks like the water washed it away."

I glanced down, surprised to see Detective Dick was right.

"Sticking your feet in the water was the unsanitary part. You do realize this lake is contaminated, correct?"

I nodded.

Shifting positions, he smiled at me. The weird way his thin lips curved over yellow teeth was worse than the accusing glare from before.

"So why did you come out here? Besides

getting wasted. Or worse. How many pills were in the bottle, and how many did you ingest?"

"Look, Detective Di...Greenwood. I don't appreciate your attitude. I'm just the person who found a dead body. I informed law enforcement, so my job as an upstanding citizen of Whitten County is done. Why I was out here and what I was doing is none of your business. Shouldn't you be figuring out the identity of the dead then notifying relatives?"

My little tirade seemed to strike a nerve. The detective's jaw clenched, snapping the straw in half.

"You might want to change your tone, Ms. Thornton. I haven't charged you with possession yet, but that doesn't mean I won't. Last time: what were you doing out here?"

I let out a sigh, unwilling to continue the conversation at the station. "Look, the last few months have been really rough on me. I lost my job, had to move in with my ex-mother-in-law, which I promise you hasn't been easy, and I don't have insurance. All the stress makes me have panic attacks. I came out here to relax and enjoy the scenery, that's all."

"And you decided to take an entire bottle of Xanax—prescribed to someone else—with you?"

I bit my lip while contemplating the best response. The body was being raised from the water. Even from the distance, I could tell it was a female. My stomach lurched, so I turned away. "There weren't many left inside. I thought, you know, I'd be in more trouble if I just pocketed a few and got caught with them on me. Having the bottle with a real prescription seemed like a good idea when I left the house."

"Well, it wasn't. It's against the law to take medication not prescribed to you. Especially a schedule four narcotic. How many did you take?"

"Not enough to wipe away the memory of seeing a dead body."

Detective Dick closed his notepad and stuck it inside his pocket. I could tell he was angry.

"Well, here are your choices, Ms. Thornton. We continue this conversation at the station *after* I take you to the hospital for a drug test, or you let one of the deputies take you home and sleep it off, then come to see me tomorrow for any follow-up questions I might have. Which one will it be?"

I should have kept my mouth shut. Should have let Detective Dick's words bounce off my skin.

Of course, I didn't. The Xanax gave me medicinal courage.

"Neither. You can't force me to take a drug test! You have no reason to, and I won't let some stranger poke me with a needle! Yeah, I took three pills to ease my frazzled mind. So what? Trying living in my shoes for a bit and see how *you* would handle it! I guarantee you, Detective, you wouldn't last an hour before grabbing something to numb the pain. I'll drive myself home, and since I gave you my address earlier, you know where to find me if you have any more fucking questions to ask."

Detective Dick yanked a set of cuffs from

his belt. Before I could move, he grabbed my arm and spun me around.

"Renee Thornton, you're under arrest for—"

"Detective? A word please?"

Clifton Simpson's voice boomed from behind me. I'd never been so grateful to hear anyone speak before.

"Not now, Deputy Simpson."

"Now, sir."

Detective Dick finished clicking the cuffs on me. From the rough pressure of his hands, my words had pissed him off. Though flying high, I decided to keep my mouth shut.

"I said not now. Take her to the station and book her on felony possession of narcotics."

My mouth dropped open.

Clifton stepped forward and whispered in the detective's ear, just loud enough for me to hear. "It's Martha Cayhill."

Detective Greenwood groaned. "How do you know for sure?"

"This," Clifton responded, holding up a soaked wallet.

"Well Christ in a bucket," Detective Greenwood muttered. "Christ in a bucket. Has anyone mentioned that little tidbit over the airwaves?"

Clifton shrugged then glanced at me. "I don't know, sir. If someone did leak it, hordes of hungry reporters will fill up the place. You'll be swarmed by lights and microphones."

Detective Greenwood raked his beefy hand across his face. "Get her outta here."

Clifton waited until the rattled detective stormed off before freeing me from the cuffs.

"Come on, I'll follow you home. You're staying with Eleanor, right?"

Rubbing my wrists, I grimaced. Small town life—God, how I hated it. Everyone knew everyone's business. "You aren't going to haul me in? Won't Detective Dick be pissed at you?"

Clifton smiled, a hint of mischief gleaming on his face. "Detective Dick? That's funny. I forgot you always had a dark sense of humor. I'm sure that isn't the first time someone's referred to him by that name. No matter. I'm following orders. He said to get you outta here, which is what I'm doing."

"Uh, yeah, he put me under arrest, remember?"

"I didn't hear him finish reading you your Miranda Rights. Did you?"

Cliff had a point. I replied with a weary smile.

"Just...don't have an accident on the way home. It'd be my ass for sure. You good to drive?"

"I'm fine, Cliff. Really. Thanks for taking it easy on me. First good thing that's happened to me in a long time. Here," I said, handing him back the coat, "appreciate you letting me use it."

Ushering me toward my car, Cliff shook his head. "Keep it. I'll pick it up tomorrow."

"Tomorrow?"

"Yeah, when I come by to ask you some more questions. After a good night's sleep, you might remember something. Wouldn't you rather I stop by? You don't seem too fond of Greenwood."

Pausing at the door, I chuckled. "I believe

the feeling is mutual. We, um, exchanged harsh words when he interrogated me before, you know, when the second Mrs. Runsford died?"

Cliff looked back toward the boardwalk. "Greenwood's not known for being a soft touch."

"Tell me something I don't know," I muttered. Afraid Cliff might use the opportunity to delve further into my volatile, previous relationship, I switched topics. "So, was that really Martha Cayhill, the mayor's wife?"

Cliff's playfulness disappeared. A sad look crossed his face. "The ID said it was. She's wearing the same outfit and ring from the missing person's poster, too. I checked."

"How long's it been since she disappeared? I can't remember. A year?"

"Sixteen months. Glad I'm not the one who's gotta tell the Mayor or answer questions from the press. It's gonna be a nightmare. The only good thing coming out of this is you'll probably get the reward money."

"Come again?"

"The Mayor offered t en thousand dollars, and the city matched it, remember? That's twenty grand for information leading to her whereabouts. In my book, that makes you the recipient. Of course, it's not my call, but if it was, I'd certainly make sure you received it."

Stunned, I really didn't know what to say. Though the money would be a blessing out of the blue, it didn't seem right to claim it. After all, it wasn't like I'd been out actively searching for the woman. Besides, just because my plans to off m yself w ere blown for the night, there would be other opportunities later to finish what I'd started. The dead didn't need money on the other side. Lights to the right caught my attention and pulled focus back to the present. "Looks like the party's about to start."

Cliff f ollowed m y g aze a nd grimaced. "Damn, someone *did* notify the vultures. Come on, let's get out of here before we're on the nightly news."

Without a word, I slunk behind the

wheel of the beat-up Chevy. After the third try, it cranked to life. Cliff's unit pulled up behind me, and we edged our way through the throng of oncoming reporters.

While driving through the dark, twisty road leading to the main highway, I felt sick to my stomach. The Xanax wasn't the only reason or the fact I'd touched a dead body. The rumbling was from the morbid connection I had with Bradford Lake. If what my mother said to me so many years ago was true—and I had no reason to doubt her after spending years trying to track down my father with no luck—the tranquil waters were his final resting place.

And Cyndi's.

Would have been mine, too, had I not discovered a body that may or may not be the Mayor of Ridgeport's missing wife.

Pulling out onto the main highway, I mentally kicked myself for picking the dirty lake to take my life. Now, instead of being able to slip away into obscurity, I was part of an investigation into the death of another person.

Life sucks, and then you die.
Or, maybe not.
At least not yet.

3

SITTING IN THE orange plastic chair normally would have made my back pound in agony but at this particular moment, my whole body was numb from shock. Funny thing, the news the doctor just brought me wasn't an immediate death sentence. No cancer or tumor floating around inside me causing the tremendous pain in my back.

Dr. Crusher had smiled while delivering

the news. "Buck up, Renee. You aren't terminally ill!"

Goody.

Dr. Crusher had a strange sense of humor. Then again, a man with such a last name who decided to become a doctor needed one. He should have gone into Orthopedics rather than general practice. That would have been hysterical. Dr. Crusher—bone surgeon. Clients would have flocked to his practice. Bet the man was hilarious at parties. Probably made his wife laugh herself into an orgasm.

No, what ailed me wasn't something that would kill me quickly. Dr. Crusher informed me I had Osteoporosis so advanced, the L4 and L5 discs in my lower back had literally disintegrated into a ticking time bomb. All the cartilage was nearly gone. The two discs had rubbed together for so long they were full of tiny cracks. If I didn't watch myself, limit certain activities, my back could crumple at any moment.

Dr. Crusher gave me a shot to help ease the discomfort and drew several vials of blood. He mentioned the lab results should be back in about one week and then I needed to schedule an appointment with a surgeon of my choice so he could forward the results.

Joy.

Not even fifty yet and my body had truly given out on me. Only fair, I guess, since my mind and soul had given up on living. The list of things Dr. Crusher informed me that I was no longer allowed to do had astounded me and made me realize how truly frail I had become.

I felt almost paralyzed as I sat on the cold plastic. I stared out the window searching, wondering if I should just leap out the window. Since my worthless bones were so brittle, the two-story fall should basically crush my insides into a pile of powder. With my luck, I would just break everything and be in excruciating pain for months and rack up more bills.

Pulling my gaze away from the window, I looked at the door. I wanted to scream. Eleanor had insisted I visit the doctor, even gave me the money for the visit. Said she was worried about my health, and after experiencing the horror of finding a dead body, wouldn't take no for an answer.

"While you're out, would you mind picking up a prescription for me at Walmart? I'm all out of Xanax," she'd asked.

I didn't mention the fact I already knew she was out of meds.

How would I explain this overwhelming sadness settling over me to Eleanor? She would laugh and say I was being dramatic. The first words out of her mouth would be something like "It's only osteoporosis for goodness sake," or something similar and that would infuriate me.

After several minutes of internal arguments between my mind and limbs about moving, I finally stood and made my way to the elevator. The appointment secretary noticed and raised her voice to catch my attention.

"Ma'am, you need to schedule your follow-up appointment."

Pressing the down button, I didn't even turn her way, I just shook my head. "I will call and make one later. When I can scrounge up the outrageous fees again."

I stepped out into the bright sunlight, grimacing at the intense light. The Indian summer from two days ago was long gone. The afternoon air was frigid.

Walking like a ninety-year-old woman, I made it to my car and eased my way down into the seat. The cold air made my back throb. A wave of anger at having to move so slowly overtook me and I threw my purse against the passenger side door. All the contents went flying.

I was a walking billboard for youth. The perfect specimen for a campaign screaming, "Kids, this is your body after forty—take care of yourself *now*!"

All the bills I had crammed into my purse were strewn across the front seat and floorboard. Thousands of dollars' worth and no way to pay them.

Leaning over, I picked up the mess. After shoving the crumpled pages back into my purse, I caught a glimpse of myself in the rear-view mirror. The past year had really taken a toll on my face. Time had trampled its way across my skin, leaving a new crop of wrinkles around my eyes and forehead.

My eyes looked dead and lifeless. Their once bright blue hue no longer held any sparkles. Although my hair was still long, the vibrancy and sheen decided to run away with the sparkle in my eyes. Instead of a pretty dark blonde, outcroppings of gray took over. I hadn't colored it in months since money was so tight.

Just like Mom used to say—mouse fur. With all that had happened to me over the years, I was surprised I had any hair at all.

Starting up the car, I headed toward the minuscule downtown area, wondering if I should just lie about my diagnosis to Eleanor. Dr. Crusher said I needed spinal surgery and gave me the name of two surgeons in Little Rock. If I told Eleanor that, she'd try to figure out a way to pay for it. Though I still had mixed feelings about the woman, and I'm pretty sure she did about me as well, I knew her well enough to know she'd want to help.

Helping me seemed to be her way of paying penance for her son's transgressions.

No way. I was already taking enough assistance from her, and I certainly wouldn't let her pay for an expensive surgery. With the cost of medical procedures, she'd have to take out a second mortgage on her house, and then we'd both be out on the streets. She was retired and on a fixed income, and too old to go back into the workforce.

Since I wasn't working and had no good leads on a job, maybe I could sell my car. The second the thought popped in my head, I laughed. Seriously, how much would a 1995 Chevy Corsica with over three-hundred thousand miles go for? I probably couldn't give the thing away.

The reward money Clifton Simpson mentioned when I found Martha Cayhill's body was a bust. I was thankful my name had been kept out of the news because the thought of dealing with reporters made me cringe. The flip side was I hadn't heard a thing from anyone, not even Detective Dick. Cliff had stopped by the next day, just like he said he would, but only to grab his jacket. The subject of Martha Cayhill never even came up. Cliff looked tired and frazzled and stayed for less than two minutes.

Why was I even worried about such things like my diagnosis or spinal surgery? Two days ago, I was ready to chuck it all and slip into the murky waters of Suicide Lake. Forty-eight hours later, I was trying to figure out a way to pay for a medical procedure I didn't want to endure.

Truly, I was a basket case. Instead of pain medication, Dr. Crusher should have given me something to sort out my brain.

Like a lobotomy.

I DIDN'T PAY much attention to my surroundings as I drove through town. I knew Ridgeport by heart. Every nook, cranny, and side-street etched into an internal map in my head. Other than a weekend getaway to Pensacola, Florida once with a few of my girlfriends from high school after my divorce, I'd spent every single day in the town. I could probably drive through it with my eyes closed and not hit a thing.

Ridgeport, Arkansas—Whitten County seat and home of the Ridgeport Lions—Class 2A football champions two years running! Woo-hoo! Population in the city limits of five-thousand, twelve-thousand if you include the entire county, according to the last census. A tiny berg situated in the middle of Nowheresville, USA. The kind of town you pass while driving on the freeway, unaware humans actually *lived* on the other side of the thick woods.

A town full of people struggling, just like me, with day-to-day life. A forgotten place firmly entrenched in old-school, good ol' boy politics and values.

Hell on earth.

I should have moved away years ago, but I didn't. Thought about it in the dark at night while crammed under the covers—alone—and even during the day at work back when I had a job. Like a fool, I remained behind, unwilling to escape for a variety of reasons. The biggest knot holding me in place was I promised myself the day I found out my mother killed my father, I wouldn't leave until I knew for sure she was telling me the truth.

In other words, I got stuck in the red clay mud, my past tethering me to the land.

"Trapped like a worm, you are," I muttered, doing my best impression of Yoda.

When I turned onto Main Street, the place was packed. People lined both sides of the two-lane road jockeying for better positions. Six news vans with their big satellite dishes were parked in front of City Hall. Slowing down, I glanced to the right and saw Mayor Peyton Cayhill standing on the concrete steps. Dressed to perfection, his expensive black suit and bright, red tie without a wrinkle or stitch out of place, he addressed the throng of reporters. His snow-white hair shimmered under the afternoon sun.

A wave of sadness hit me. Poor man. At

his age, losing a loved one was hard enough when the cause was natural. Normal. Living the last sixteen months in a constant state of worry and fear, hoping and praying she'd turn up—alive—had to have been mental torture. Mayor Cayhill had the extra baggage of dealing with the fact his wife's disappearance was under investigation for murder.

Murder!

In this small town?

When the ten-o'clock news reported the jaw-dropping story yesterday evening, I was stunned. There hadn't been a murder in Whitten County since my ex-husband killed his wife, which was almost six years ago. The next one was over thirty years in the past—the night my mother killed my dad and his lover. No one knew about that secret, so the town was in a state of collective mourning for the horrible ending to their beloved First Lady. Prior to that, you had to go way back to the early 1950s. Mom told me the story once how a botched moonshine transaction ended when the seller killed the buyer after a disagreement over pricing. Lack of major crimes occurring was the main reason most people born in the community stayed.

Safety.

The creepy factor of my ties to three-out-of-four murders made my head spin.

Even Dr. Crusher mentioned the tragedy during the examination. "You know, I went to school with Martha, Peyton, and of course, your mother. Oh, they were such a lovely couple! No finer l ady e ver graced Whitten County. There wasn't a charity or community service Martha wasn't a member of. To think someone ended her life is worse than thinking she just up and ran off!"

Everyone knew and everyone was talking about it. I played the role of a shocked citizen to perfection and never mentioned my involvement in the discovery.

After all, I knew how to keep secrets. I had over thirty years of practice.

I considered stopping to listen to the news conference but opted to head to Walmart and pick up Eleanor's Xanax. I had prescription pain meds of my own to fill though I knew I wouldn't. Not that I didn't want them, I simply didn't have much money left to buy them. I'd sold everything I had of value, including my old computer, all my DVDs and CDs, even my treasured collection of snow globes. Out of the little haul, I had less than five-hundred dollars left in my wallet.

I could watch the Mayor's interview on the news later. The need to soak in a hot bath called to me, for it was the only thing I could do to ease the pain in my back that was free.

I pulled into the parking lot at Walmart and went inside. While waiting for the pharmacist, I thought about Martha Cayhill—and Mom. Martha graduated a year after my mother and had also been homecoming queen. Mom had been a beautiful woman. When drunk, she'd spend hours staring at grainy images of her younger self, urging me to look along with her while she reveled in her glory days. Caroline Clark was gorgeous. Curvy. Sexy. A vivacious, come-hither smile perpetually on her lips.

Martha Cayhill was different. She was beautiful, too, but in an opposite way. Mom was Ridgeport's Marilyn Monroe, and Martha was its Jackie O. Tall, stately, serene, with big brown eyes and full lips—she could have passed as Jackie's sister. She was the kind of woman meant to be on the arm of a politician—just like Mrs. Kennedy.

Mom *hated* Martha. When flipping through her yearbook, she had no choice but to look at a woman she considered her nemesis. Mom had been head cheerleader and Martha was on the squad, too. Martha had been a junior maid the year Mom was crowned homecoming queen. All of Mom's fond memories of being the "it" girl in high school shared the same space as Martha.

Once, I made the mistake of asking Mom why she despised Martha so much. Her answer, spoken in a heavy, drunken words, still made my skin crawl.

"That bitch never had to work for a thing! I did. I wasn't born into money. I worked hard for every accomplishment. Martha didn't. Daddy's money bought her way into things and titles I scratched and clawed my way up.

Privileged bitch. She didn't appreciate the accolades because they were handed to her. Mine were earned, and they meant the world to me. The only thing I trumped her at was marrying your father. He was captain of the football team, you know. Everyone wanted him, including Martha. She had to settle for the slimy little worm, Peyton."

Peyton Cayhill was elected Mayor three months before Dad's disappearance. Mom never said a word about it. She didn't have to voice her opinions. They were expressed just fine after she took an ink pen and scratched out every occurrence of Martha Cayhill's face in the yearbook.

"Ma'am, your medication's ready."

Pulled back to the present by the perky voice of the pharmacy technician, I walked up to the counter. While scrounging around for the remaining cash Eleanor had given me, the piece of paper Dr. Crusher wrote my prescription out on fell out. Before I could pick it back up, the young woman had it in her hands.

"Oh, you have another one? Okay, give me a few minutes."

"No, uh, I can't afford to fill it right now," I said, reaching my hand out.

The look of pity on the woman's face made me want to punch her in the mouth.

"No insurance, huh? That's okay. This medication comes in generic form, too. Ten dollars. Can you do that?"

Snickers and whispers from people in line behind me made my face flush with embarrassment. Unsure what to say to make the situation easier and less painful, I simply nodded.

Standing there at the pharmacy counter of Walmart, I wanted to crawl behind a shelf and disappear. The bright fluorescent bulbs above felt like hot stage lights illuminating my shame and humiliation. The tension in my muscles didn't help the pain in my back. I closed my eyes and took a deep cleansing breath, forcing myself to remain still instead of fleeing the store.

Like I could run, anyway. The lumbering gait would make the people behind me cackle with delight.

"Girl, can you believe it was murder? I mean, in our town? You best remember to start locking your doors at night. The world just ain't a safe place anymore. Not at all."

The words of a woman behind me helped calm my frazzled nerves. It seemed she and the person were no longer interested in the poor chick, standing in front of them, who couldn't afford her meds.

"No doubt! To think, all the time spent searching for her and there she was, floating around in Suicide Lake. Tragic! Bill's already installed an extra set of deadbolts on the front and back doors. Tomorrow, he's meeting a guy out in Poyen to buy a trained guard dog. Said he don't want me staying at home alone while he works nights. He's such a thoughtful man. You should check into that, Gretchen. Getting a dog to keep you safe."

"I'll do no such thing, Charlene! I've been alone for years now after Walter passed on, and I don't want to share my living space with some creature full of fleas and in need of constant supervision. I've got my protection right at my bedside. Name's Smith & Wesson."

"Good for you! Always knew you was a smart gal. So, have you heard any more tidbits you want to share? The news ain't saying much."

Despite the fact I hated gossip, my ears perked up. Even without turning around to look at her face, I recognized the voice of one of the women.

Gretchen Chase.

She'd been my immediate supervisor at the call center—and the one who'd let me go. Gretchen's husband had been one of the three lawyers in town before he collapsed on the floor of the courthouse after suffering a heart attack during the sentencing phase of my ex-husband's trial. He died on the polished wooden floor in front of a stunned courtroom.

Though the subject was never broached at work, after Gretchen's husband died, our long-standing friendship vanished. We became nothing more than supervisor/employee. There was a faint niggling in the back of my mind that Gretchen somehow blamed me for her husband's death. Blamed probably wasn't the right word. Maybe *associated* me with the loss of her spouse. Whatever the reason for the demise of our relationship, it happened.

Carl Chase's connections throughout town allowed him to be privy to even the faintest whisper of gossip. Apparently, Gretchen still had access. Pushing aside my previous embarrassment, I honed in on their conversation. Since Gretchen was about to drop a load of privileged information, she lowered her voice. Ignoring the other noises in the store, I strained my ears to listen.

"Oh, yes. Enough to make your hair stand on end."

"Do tell!"

"Ol' Martha Cayhill didn't kill herself at Suicide Lake."

"That ain't anything new, girl! News

59

already said a homicide investigation is underway."

"I know. Obviously, you missed my point. She didn't commit suicide at the lake, and she didn't *die* at the lake, either. Martha was killed somewhere else then dumped in the water. Recently."

The other woman named Charlene gasped in shock. It took everything I had not to do the same.

"What? How do they know that already?"

"Because she still had flesh o n h er *and* they found evidence she'd been trussed up like a hog waiting for the slaughter truck. She's been gone for over sixteen months, which means she'd been nothing but a pile of bones by now, had she been killed back then. The coroner said she'd been in the water less than a week."

"Lord-a-mercy! Wonder where she's been all this time?"

"Girl, you know Martha. She could've been anywhere doing God-only-knows-what. The woman certainly wasn't a white lily like everyone likes to picture her. Not at all."

The young girl popped back over with my medicine. Unwilling to turn around and face the annoying gossip queens, I paid for the pills in silence, thankful the girl hadn't used my name.

"Renee? Is that you?"

Damn.

Without turning around, I nodded. "Afternoon, Gretchen."

"Since you're out in the middle of the day, guess you haven't found a job yet. Rest assured if anyone calls me, I'll make sure to give you a reference."

The nasty tone in Gretchen's voice sent sparks of anger throughout my chest. All sorts of ugly comebacks bounced inside my head. Saying anything would require me to face her, and I just couldn't bring myself to do it. At that very moment, I realized Gretchen Chase, nee Snowden, had turned into my personal nemesis.

One of Mom's favorite sayings popped

up inside my head: "Love and hate—only the span of a butterfly's wings between them."

The anger overrode my shame. I spun around and let Gretchen have it. "Will that reference come with a warning about your prejudices toward me for something completely out of my control? Oh, and the fact we used to be friends but you turned on me for no reason other than you're a cold-hearted, gossiping, backstabbing bitch?"

All the color drained from Gretchen's face then rushed back. White to beet red in the blink of an eye. I'd never seen someone's eyes open up so big. From behind me, I heard the girl at the counter gasp. Charlene's hand flew to her mouth.

Rather than wait for Gretchen to compose herself and slam me with a witty retort, I left. In minutes, I was back at my little hunk-o-rust and on my way to Eleanor's.

With a big smile on my face. I wasn't one to stand up for myself—my ex made sure to beat that thought out of me during the course of our marriage. It worked, too, because I never even had the guts to leave him. I'd been thoroughly warned by his fists not to try. He'd left me for another woman.

The warden freed the prisoner—the weak one who never attempted to escape.

Seeing Gretchen again dredged up painful memories of my past so I blocked them and concentrated on the information she'd provided, rather than the personal connection.

I knew it was wrong to be intrigued by what I'd just heard, yet I couldn't help it. The tragic ending of Martha Cayhill's life burrowed under my skin for some reason. Maybe it was because I felt connected to her somehow since I found her body. Maybe it was because I wanted to believe someone like Martha—a woman who seemed to have it all—could have been just as lonely and depressed as I was and opted to end her life.

Or maybe it was because I was just plain nosy.

Whatever the reason, the death of Martha Cayhill brought back enough spark into my dim world to keep me around.

At least long enough to find o ut what happened to her and why.

4

ELEANOR SAT IN the old rocking chair on the porch, busy reading the newspaper. The minute I drove up, she tossed the paper aside and walked down the steps to the driveway. The look of anticipation and eagerness to hear the results of my visit with Dr. Crusher made me wince.

"I was starting to get worried. What took you so long?"

"Sorry. Took me a while to get through

downtown. The place was packed full of reporters."

Eleanor looked aghast as we walked toward the house. I took the stairs carefully, pretending to look for something in my purse as I motioned for her to go first. Once inside, I handed her the sack with her pills then sat on the couch.

"Thanks for picking these up," Eleanor said after setting the package on the table. She retreated to the kitchen, mumbling as she walked. "Let me get you a fresh glass of tea and then you can tell me what Dr. Crusher said."

Since Eleanor couldn't see me, I rolled my eyes. In seconds, she was back with two full glasses of orange-lemon tea. Her favorite, not mine.

"Thanks, Eleanor. Visit went fine. The pain in my back is from a pulled muscle. Dr. Crusher said to take things easy for a while, alternate hot and cold packs, and plenty of hot showers. Gave me a prescription for muscle relaxers, too. Might take a week or so before I'm pain-free."

I could tell from the disapproving look on Eleanor's wrinkled face she didn't buy my story. Guess my skills at lying were slipping.

"Well, that's good to hear. At least it isn't something permanent."

Eleanor wasn't a very good liar, either. I decided to change the subject before she pressed me for additional information.

"Ran into Gretchen Chase while filling your prescription. She had some interesting things to say about Martha Cayhill."

Eleanor waved a dismissive hand in the air. "That woman's *always* got something to say. Surprised she hasn't choked on a bug as much as that mouth of hers flaps. Never understood why you two were friends. She may have money to buy expensive clothes, but that don't mean her heart is pretty."

"Oh, I agree with you one-hundred percent. She's certainly not one of my favorite people in this town. Doesn't change the fact about what she said in terms of Martha."

Grimacing, Eleanor set the glass of tea on the table next to her and let out a sigh. Her gaze settled on the empty spot where family pictures used to sit. One of me and her son at our wedding; one of our son, William; and one of her son's second wedding. I was so glad she removed them after I moved in. Though few, Eleanor did possess some positive qualities.

"Rumors spread around this place so fast makes my head spin. What did the old bitty have to say?" she asked.

"That Martha was killed somewhere else and recently dumped into the lake. Oh, and hinted Martha Cayhill wasn't the saint she painted herself out to be."

"Ain't no one alive in this world that's close to being the person they portray in public, so that's not news. Why does she think Martha was killed somewhere else? News and paper ain't mentioned anything like that."

"She said Martha had marks on her that looked like she'd been tied up. Don't know whether that part's true, but the other part she mentioned certainly is. I know because I saw it with my own eyes."

"What part?"

"She still had flesh on her. If she died over a year ago, she wouldn't."

Eleanor looked out the window. For a few moments, she didn't speak. I could tell she was struggling with what to say next. The muscles in her throat tightened and her thin lips pursed together. When she was in deep concentration, the resemblance to her son was downright eerie.

"You're a strong woman, Renee. If I'da seen a dead body, well, I don't know how I'd react. At my age, I'm sure a heart attack would follow."

Taking a drink of tea to settle my own nerves, I wondered what hidden meaning the comment held. "Trust me, I freaked. Damn near fell off the boardwalk and into the water right next to her. I'm sure I'll have nightmares for weeks."

Eleanor turned her face away from the window. Her cloudy green eyes scanned my face. Confusion and a hint of irritation replaced the sad look from seconds before. "I still don't understand what you were doing out at Suicide Lake. It's dirty and I don't just mean the water. The ground's tainted from all the blood shed there over the years. Too many secrets hiding underneath the water. Wouldn't have surprised me if you'd seen a ghost or two."

I couldn't stop the eye-roll at that comment. "Eleanor, there are no such things as ghosts."

"You have your opinion, I have mine. Either way, the place ain't safe—especially for a woman alone. What if you had fallen into the water and drowned?"

The conversation was taking a turn I didn't like so I stood. "But I didn't. Like I said that night, I just needed some time to contemplate things. The lake may be a cesspool but it is still beautiful at sunset. After what happened, I promise you I'll never go back. Thanks for the tea, Eleanor. If you'll excuse me, I'm going to take a hot shower like Dr. Crusher suggested."

I only made it to the doorway leading toward the bedrooms when Eleanor said, "I forgot to tell you. Detective Greenwood stopped by about an hour before you got home. He asked for you to call him when you returned. Said he needs to ask you a few more questions."

Joy. So much for fading away into the woodwork. I couldn't fathom what else there was left to ask me.

"Renee, before you take a shower, you might want to put your car in the garage. I noticed some strange vehicles driving by the house real slow earlier. Might be someone from the mortgage company or a process server skulking around."

The stacks of green Certified Mail cards on the table insisting I come to the post office to pick up a registered letter sat on the counter. Eleanor was probably correct, for the foreclosure sale of my house was only weeks away. Grabbing the keys from my purse, I headed outside.

The temperature had dropped significantly from only minutes earlier. According to the six a.m. news, a chance of freezing rain and sleet before nine p.m. was likely. Yay! More cold weather to aggravate my bones.

After pulling the car in the garage, I decided to ask Eleanor if she would allow me to take her laptop into my room so I could search for jobs while resting on the bed. It wasn't exactly a lie because I certainly would peruse the skimpy classified l istings, which would take me all of five minutes.

What I really wanted to do—uninterrupted—was search the Internet to see what various news sites were reporting about Martha Cayhill. If what Gretchen "Motor-Mouth" Chase said was true, surely some nosy reporter had sniffed out the truth and plastered it in cyberspace.

"GLAD YOU'RE HOME, Ms. Thornton. We need to talk."

Jerking at the sound of Detective Greenwood's voice from behind me made pain shoot through my lower back. "You really shouldn't sneak up on people like that, Detective. Bad manners."

"So is not returning a phone call when requested."

Stopping at the edge of the steps, I glowered at Detective Dick. "I just got here. Didn't you see me pulling into the garage?"

"Actually, no. I was on the phone. Things have been hectic the last forty-eight hours. Working a homicide isn't easy."

He looked beyond tired. Bone weary, like me. With a casual glance, I noticed he wore the same outfit he had on two days ago. The stubble was thicker and instead of a straw, his fingers fiddled with an unlit cigarette.

"As I told Mrs. Runsford, I have some items to discuss with you. You'll need to come with me."

Panic tore through my chest at the look on his face. Was he going to finish what he started at the lake and arrest me? Damn! I could just picture the look of repugnance on Eleanor's face when she came to bail me out of jail—if she opted to spring me.

Dandy. A perfect end to a perfect day. Why didn't I just jump in the lake when I had the chance?

"I don't understand why you can't just talk to me here, Detective. I'm very tired and in pain. My doctor said—"

"It won't take long. There are some papers that need to be signed, and I didn't bring them with me."

Oh shit, he was going to arrest me. I sighed. "How much will the bail be? I'll need to tell Eleanor."

Detective Greenwood put the cigarette to his lips and lit it. The flame illuminated the deep creases in his forehead and cheeks. "I'm not arresting you, Ms. Thornton. We just need you to come to the station."

"We?"

Nodding his head toward the unmarked unit at the edge of the driveway, Detective Greenwood responded, "Mayor Cayhill would like to speak with you. I'll wait why you grab a jacket."

Following his gaze, I looked at the sedan. Sure enough, Peyton Cayhill sat in the front seat. Stunned, unable to think of a plausible reason why I couldn't go, I motioned for him to wait, turned and went inside.

"I see he didn't feel like waiting for you to call him back. What's going on, Renee?" Eleanor asked, looking up from her perch at the kitchen table.

Snatching up my jacket, annoyed at the fact the woman didn't miss a damn thing, I responded, "Detective Greenwood said I need to go with him and sign a statement or something. Shouldn't take too long."

"Okay. I'll fix you a plate and put it in the microwave. Um, hope you don't mind, but I turned on the computer to check the weather. Noticed you had an email about a job, so I clicked on it. Hopefully, Detective Greenwood won't keep you too long because you'll need to respond back and confirm. Looks like you have an interview tomorrow at ten at the Mayor's office."

I let my irritation at Eleanor's snooping slide. It wasn't the first time she'd stuck her nose in my email account, and probably wouldn't be the last. Considering I only used email as a way to let prospective employers contact me about a job and nothing else, it wasn't like she'd find anything embarrassing.

"I don't understand. I never applied for a job with the city!"

"Well, one can't look a gift horse in the mouth, right? Maybe it's the Mayor's way of thanking you for finding his wife."

My previous hesitation about getting into a vehicle with Detective Greenwood and the Mayor disappeared. Was it possible my shitty luck just changed? Did I dare even hope? A job with the city would certainly pay more than the call center, and the hours would be wonderful. No shift work. Maybe the salary would be enough, and in time, I could catch up on some back payments and get my house out of foreclosure.

"I'll be back soon, Eleanor. Promise."

"Good, because I fixed c hicken and dumplings for supper. It's best when fresh, not reheated."

Detective Greenwood stood by the driver's door, smoke billowing around his head like freight train steam. When he saw me exit the front door, he took one last drag and tossed the butt across the yard. He opened the back door and held it wide.

"Ms. Thornton, good to see you again."

Unsure what to say to the man, I forced a smile and stuck out my hand. Mayor Cayhill clasped it and I suppressed the urge to cringe. His hand was slick, full of too much oil or lotion, and grip forceful. He must have noticed my unease because he graced me with a comforting smile.

"I'm sorry if Detective Greenwood hasn't fully explained my riding along with him this afternoon. For one, I needed to get away from those dreadful reporters. The second reason is because I wanted to thank you in person. You've given me some closure to a very painful chapter of my life."

Words finally formed and escaped my dry throat. "I'm sorry for your loss, sir."

Detective Greenwood slid into the driver's seat and fired up the car. After backing out and pulling onto the main road, Mayor Cayhill answered, "One person's loss is another person's gain, Ms. Thornton."

He turned back around and faced the front. Not another word was spoken inside the car during the remainder of the ten-minute drive to the building housing Whitten County Sheriff's Office.

WHITTEN COUNTY SHERIFF'S Office was the second biggest building in the city. The largest was the jail, which sat in all its concrete glory sprawled across ten acres of prime farmland. The new building that housed Whitten County's law enforcement agency had been built less than five years ago. A big, marble sign the size of a small vehicle sat in the middle of the landscaped lawn, welcoming all visitors with the words, *Whitten County – A Perfect Place to Call Home.*

Detective Dick parked in a spot by the front and then exited the car. So did the Mayor. I tried to open the door to follow but was locked inside. A wave of paranoia hit me. I'd never been inside a police vehicle before and felt like a criminal. When the detective opened the door, I breathed a sigh of relief.

"Right this way, Ms. Thornton."

The man's attitude was completely different than the night at the lake. I needed to consider a different nickname. Detective Limp Dick popped into my head and I almost laughed. The humor of the thought disappeared when I noticed a long set of steps looming in front of me. I dreaded making my way up them. Climbing stairs was an activity that aggravated my back. Biting my lip, I grabbed the handrail and forced myself to keep up with their pace.

Once inside, a rush of warm air ruffled my hair. The heat was a welcome break from the blustery cold outside. Arkansas winters were usually mild but when the temperature did dip below the freezing mark, it was bone-chilling. The always-present moisture in the air went through a coat like you weren't even wearing one.

While walking down a long hallway to what I assumed would lead to Detective L.D.'s office, we passed by Cliff Simpson. I smiled but Cliff didn't even look in my direction. I wondered if he'd been reprimanded for not taking me into custody. Even though I was several steps behind the detective, I felt the shift in his demeanor. Agitation rolled off the man in waves. We all passed each other as though strangers in a big city.

"Here we are, Ms. Thornton. Please, have a seat."

He motioned to a chair across from a small desk. Mayor Cayhill moved past me and stood near the window. After shuffling through stacks of paper on the desk, the detective found the file he was looking for and opened it up.

The man looked as comfortable as I felt.

"Would you like something to drink?" Mayor Cayhill asked.

"Uh, no, I'm fine," I muttered.

"I'd like some coffee to help warm these old bones. Would you mind, Detective?"

I'm sure Detective Richard Greenwood had never fetched coffee for anyone other than himself. He was the fetchor not the fetchee. The look on his face at being asked to perform such a trivial task was hysterical. To his credit, he didn't say a word as he stood and left the office.

Before the door was even shut, Mayor Cayhill took over the detective's spot behind the desk. With practiced ease, he smoothed imaginary wrinkles in his tie and smiled at me. I'd never been in such close proximity to him so I studied his face. Dark blue eyes edged in gray eyelashes stared back at me. His white hair was wavier up close. His skin was wrinkled but like most men, age made him look distinguished, not old and frumpy. Warmth and charm oozed from him. I understood why the man picked politics as his livelihood.

He still looked remarkably close to the pictures in the yearbook I recalled from my youth. He graduated the year before Mom, so he had to be in his late sixties. Other than the white hair, he sure didn't look it. To calm my nerves, I pictured him at home, standing in front of a huge mirror, applying some expensive cream to keep his skin soft and supple.

Lacing his fingers together, Mayor Cayhill took a deep breath. "As I mentioned before, Ms. Thornton, I asked Detective Greenwood to bring you here so I could thank you in person. I'm sure what you...experienced at Bradford Lake was difficult."

"It was, but certainly not as difficult as what you must be going through. Again, I'm so sorry for your loss. I didn't know her personally, but your wife seemed like such a lovely person."

"She was, indeed. No finer woman in this state than my Martha. That's why I just can't fathom why anyone would want to harm her. It just makes no sense to me, and I'm a man who deals in sense. Logic. Black and white. I'm having trouble grappling with the senselessness of it all."

"I can't imagine. Again, I'm so sorry."

Mayor Cayhill paused. He looked down at the file folder in front of him then over at me. A subtle hint of tears glistened in his eyes. He blinked twice and they disappeared.

"I'm sure you're wondering why we brought you here, Renee. May I call you Renee?"

"The thought has crossed my mind, sir. And yes, of course."

"Please, call me Peyton. After all, we have a connection now, don't we?"

Yeah, a morbid one. "One I'm sure neither of us ever wanted."

"Very true, Renee. Very true. So, let's get down to why you're here. Are you aware there's a reward for information leading to my wife's whereabouts? Ten thousand from me and an additional ten thousand from the city?"

I couldn't think of the right words to say so I nodded.

"Well, I'm sorry to say you'll only be receiving my portion. There's a reason for that, so what I'm about to say needs to stay in this room. May I have your word?"

Swallowing twice to dislodge the lump in my throat, I whispered, "Of course."

"Part of being a good leader is to have the ability to read people. I knew right away you were trustworthy. Honest. Solid and dependable. The backbone of our little piece of Heaven here in Whitten County, if you will."

Politician—born and bred. Jackie certainly married JFK. Peyton Cayhill was smooth, confident, and full of shit. But hey, it seemed he was offering me manna from above in the form of ten grand—and maybe a job, too?—so I kept my mouth shut.

Mayor Cayhill looked down at the papers in front of him again. "I'm sure you're aware I went to school with your mother and father? And that I'm thoroughly acquainted with Billy Runsford?"

Again, I nodded, wondering where in the Hell this conversation was going. So far, it was all over the place. I tried, but couldn't imagine what in the world my parents and my ex—God, he said his freaking name!—had to do with all this.

"Our town and community are growing, and it doesn't need any more scrutiny from the prying eyes of outsiders while we move forward toward a better future. That is the reason your name has been kept out of all this. We didn't want the reporters to link you to the discovery of Martha's body."

Aha! The proverbial light bulb burst inside my mind. "Because it could lead back to...my ex."

Mayor Cayhill smiled. This time, it wasn't warm. Or inviting. It was downright eerie.

"Exactly! I'm sure you know people who don't reside in less populated communities tend to assume negative things about small town living. You must admit, this is a strange twist of events. A man brutally beat his second wife to death and then the first wife discovers the body of the town's Mayor. Bad publicity no matter how much we stand from the rooftops and shout it was mere coincidence."

"Are you worried people would think we're hiding something, is that it?"

"Yes, even though we aren't. Also, since I plan on writing a letter to the Parole Board, asking them to deny Billy's parole request next month, it might be construed by those who'd like to see him released we were somehow...oh, what's the word? Cahoots? Yes, in cahoots together."

My stomach dropped and I felt dizzy. This wasn't happening. Did I hear him right? Did he just suavely throw in a veiled bribe?

Mayor Cayhill seemed to have noticed my distress. Clearing his throat, he continued. "Have you...discussed what happened out at Bradford Lake with anyone?"

I bit my lip, unsure if I should fib or come clean. Deciding I didn't want to drag Eleanor into the web of lies between me and the Mayor, I lied. "No. I was so...upset I just haven't been able to talk about it."

"Quite understandable. Good to hear.

Like I mentioned, I knew you were dependable. Strong, too, to endure such an awful experience on your own."

"I'm no stranger to difficulties, sir."

Mayor Cayhill gave a slight nod of understanding. The eerie smile from seconds ago morphed into a warm grin. "Peyton, remember?"

"Sorry, guess I'm just a little stunned by all this. Peyton. Got it."

"I'm aware of your past struggles, and that's part of the reason the decision was made to leave your name out of the report. No one will know you were out there, which is why the city will not pay any reward to you. I, however, will. Again, just between the two of us. I've known your kin since childhood—it's the right thing to do. You've lived through some very trying times, Renee. It saddens me to think it took my own personal tragedy to open my eyes to the suffering of others in the town I love."

Despite the fact I didn't agree with his reasons or the bribe about my ex, the thought of having that much cash made my heart pound with glee. It was only five grand shy of paying off my entire mortgage!

"Thank you," was all I could say.

"There is one other item I'd like to discuss before you leave."

Mayor Cayhill picked up an envelope and handed it to me. My hands shook as I took the wad of cash I assumed held ten thousand dollars. The pesky lump of tears formed in my throat again so I choked out, "Okay."

"It's my understanding your house is in foreclosure. I believe the reward money will make sure you retain your home. And since I made the decision to deprive you of the city's portion of the reward, I came up with a better plan. Detective Greenwood informed me you were searching for a job, so I'd like to extend the offer to work in my office. Can you start tomorrow?"

Overcome with emotion, the tears came. I didn't want them to, but they didn't listen to my internal pleas to remain inside my eyes. Even though Mayor Cayhill's reasons were ridiculous and I didn't buy a word of his impassioned speech, he just changed my life.

A life I'd planned on ending days before. The man had no idea he'd just offered a lifeline to a woman drowning in her own suicide lake.

Clearing my throat, I grinned through the tears. "Yes, sir. What time?"

6

IT WAS AFTER six-thirty p.m. when Detective Greenwood dropped me off at Eleanor's. My previous interest in watching Mayor Cayhill's interview on the news no longer a concern. I had a front row, special VIP performance up close and personal less than twenty minutes earlier. I'd been privy to things the press would cut off an appendage to hear.

Things that would make Gretchen Chase *drool*.

Ol' peppy Detective L.D. didn't say one word—and neither did I—after we left the Sheriff's department. What was there to say? He had to have known what was going on, and what Mayor Cayhill offered me, so why discuss it? I'm sure in his book, I won and he lost. I certainly wouldn't have to worry any longer about being arrested for being barred out at the lake.

After his unit disappeared from the street, I stood at the edge of the drive and stared at Eleanor's three-bedroom house. Cute. Quaint. Taken care of despite its age. Similar in design and style to my house. Hanging baskets full of fake plants dotted the corners of the porch. A weathered lawn ornament reading *Bloom Where God Plants You* leaned against a leafless oak tree.

Eleanor had lived in the house ever since she married Kyle Runsford. Had he not succumbed to prostate cancer fifteen years ago, their golden wedding anniversary would have been celebrated next month. Eleanor and I shared many common things, and another was she remained single since the passing of her husband.

Of course, I remained single and my bed colder than the current freezing temps for a different reason than Eleanor. Numerous times in the past, she'd drop comments about missing the love of her life and how no man could replace Kyle in her heart—blah, blah, and blah.

Wow, as I neared the half-century mark, I'd turned into a hardcore cynic. Another one of Mom's descriptions of me come to fruition. Poor. White trash. Cynical.

I didn't begrudge Eleanor's loving relationship with Kyle or anyone else in the world who had someone they connected with in such an intimate way. Quite the opposite: I was green with envy. Pea-freaking-green. I wanted, no *craved* to have someone to love. Dreamt about it for so many years—yearned for it every time I watched a sappy love story on TV or read a romance. Wanted someone to sweep me off my feet, gather me into strong arms, whisper in my ear his undying love more than *anything*.

Instead, life handed me a man who knocked me off m y f eet, c hoked m e with strong arms, and whispered death threats in my ear.

Ah, so much for love.

Usually, when I let my weak yearnings rattle around in my head, I cried. Not today! For the first t ime i n—oh, p retty much ever—I had hope. Something to look forward to besides downing a bottle of pills and slipping below dark water. In one day, literally less than thirty minutes, my entire world shifted, sending me in a direction I never imagined even in my most vivid dreams.

Now, I had to figure o ut h ow t o inform Eleanor without telling her the truth. Oh, and convince her not to say anything to anybody about what I'd told her before. The old expression about having to tell thousands of lies to hide just one was certainly on the mark.

Maybe instead of lying, it was time to tell

the truth. She was, after all, the only semblance of a family I had left. She'd provided me a warm place to stay, kept me fed, given me money to see the doctor. I owed her honesty, not a package of lies. The woman's sharp eyes would see right through my tall tales anyway.

What did I have to lose? If Mayor Cayhill ever found out I'd lied to him, what could he do to me? Fire me? Ask for the money back? He wouldn't risk exposing the secrets for fear I'd open my mouth and set things straight. If he truly was a man who saw things logically and in black and white, he'd probably already figured that into his calculations before handing me a wad of cash.

I wouldn't lie. Eleanor Runsford deserved better than that. She, too, had suffered losses in her life, yet was still kind enough—whatever her personal motivations were—to extend kindness to another person in need.

Groaning, I climbed up the stairs, marveling at how even a short amount of time and a bit of money had the power to change one's heart. With one last, deep breath, I stepped inside the door and called out to Eleanor.

"I JUST DON'T know what to say. I'm stunned."

Eleanor wasn't lying. I'd never seen her look so shocked, not even when Kyle passed away or after her son was sentenced to fifteen years down in Pine Bluff. Her green eyes were wide pools of disbelief. I'd told her everything except the part about the Mayor writing a letter to keep my ex in prison.

"I know exactly how you feel. Almost fell out of the chair in the detective's office. Still haven't processed it all myself, either. I mean, one minute, I'm standing in Walmart, panicked because I was about to spend money I really didn't have to spare, and the next, I have a way out of debt and a job. Cue the *Twilight Zone* theme."

Eleanor chewed on her bottom lip while staring at her lap. A shadow of concern spread across her face. "I understand Mayor Cayhill giving you the reward money. I do. You found his wife, which was what it was for. But those reasons for wanting to keep your name out of the whole thing *and* giving you a job? Fishy. Way too fishy. He wants something from you. No one is that nice. Not when it comes to cash."

I finished the last bite of chicken and dumplings, nodding in agreement. "I got that impression, too, though I have no idea what it could be. Maybe we're both so jaded we're reading more into than we should."

"Jaded—yes. Stupid? No. Anyone with a computer or ability to research documents at the library could pull up some of the town's sordid past. What happened with Billy was all over the news, too. So was the incident back when I was a young girl. The mayor can't wash away the connection simply by leaving your name out of a report. Even if he does manage to keep a lid on certain...things from others, people around here will still know. They'll put two-and-two together. You moving back home and with a new job at the same time? Oh, yes. Mouths will flap. Like I said earlier, rumors spread fast in this town."

"Eleanor, I appreciate your concerns. Have a bundle of them myself. People have been yammering about me since I was a kid. Let them. It's nothing new. Something else will catch their attention soon enough and they'll forget all about me."

Nodding once, Eleanor stood and walked across the living room. She took the empty plate from my hands and headed to the kitchen. I followed, eager to take a pain pill and call it a night.

After depositing the dish in the sink, Eleanor turned around and looked at me. An air of sadness and worry made her look older than her actual years. "Renee, I know we've had our differences in the past, but I hope you know how much you mean to me. I've enjoyed having someone to take care of. Made the house feel like a home again. It may sound corny, but at my age, I'm supposed to be corny. You're like the daughter I never had. I didn't care for Billy's second wife though I certainly didn't wish for her life to end. I would have preferred a simple divorce, but my preferences didn't happen. What I'm saying is, I love you, and I'm worried. My gut tells me this is wrong."

How many times could my brain handle being stunned in one day? Eleanor could have just said she was the queen of an alien race, sent to save all of Earth before destroyed by a meteor, and I wouldn't have been more shocked.

Tears filled her eyes so Eleanor turned away, fiddling with the lone dish in the sink. "I gave my word I won't say a thing, and I intend to keep it. All bets are off, though, if something happens to you. Then, I'll call every reporter in this state and ruin that bastard. Guaranteed."

Unsure what to say, I moved closer, placing my hand on her thin shoulder. Eleanor flinched then relaxed as a bond I didn't realize had been there before intensified. " Thank y ou, E leanor. For everything. I...love you, too. Goodnight."

I left the kitchen and went to the bedroom. Before closing the door, I glanced at the one shut across from it.

Billy's room.

Saying his name, really looking at the area he'd occupied for years before we married, something inside me changed. The internal levy I'd built years ago to protect me from crumbling, burst. Floodwaters of emotion washed over me.

I wouldn't let Eleanor hear me cry, so I shut the door and headed to the bathroom. The noise of the shower would cover my sobs.

A HORRIBLE NIGHTMARE woke me up. The pillow was soaked with tears and my arms sore from gripping the sheets. Shaking my head to clear the thoughts away, I sat and flipped the bedside lamp on. The dim light didn't help remove the remaining images. The skeletons of my father and Cyndi bobbed on the lake, their watery, garbled voices called out for me to join them.

I knew nightmares would come, but I expected them to be about finding Martha. The dreams about my father and his whore used to invade my mind years ago. They started after the doctor at Arkansas Center for Mental Care forced me to take some strong narcotic to calm me down after I lost William. Thora-something-or-other. After a year of outpatient counseling, the nightmares stopped.

For a while.

They came back when Billy starting beating me less than six months later. Apparently, our child dying was my fault, and I had to pay for it.

In blood.

Lots and lots of blood. And bruises. Broken bones. Death threats.

I shouldn't have taken the pain pill. Maybe it was in the same category or family of drugs like the other. They may or may not be the reason the terrifying dreams reappeared, but just in case they were, I decided to flush t he r emaining l ittle white terrors down the toilet.

Mission accomplished, I clicked off the light in the bathroom and padded back to bed. When I reached for the comforter, a noise from outside the window caught my attention. Pushing back the thin curtains, I gasped.

Outside the window stood Cliff Simpson in his uniform. At the edge of the driveway sat his patrol unit, white tendrils of smoke pluming from the exhaust. He motioned for me to come outside. Glancing at the alarm clock, I squinted to read the time.

Two-thirty a.m.

Curious as to why he was here, I motioned for him to hang on and let the curtain fall back. Grabbing my robe and sliding on a pair of worn-out slippers, I slipped out of the bedroom and padded down the hall to the front door. Eleanor was a heavy sleeper, but even so, I made sure to make no noise and mind my steps on the creaky front porch.

Cliff had moved from the window and stood next to the hood of his vehicle. I walked over and joined him, glad the weatherman was wrong and it was only cold. No freezing rain or sleet. "Haven't seen you in years and this is twice now in two days. What're doing here, Cliff?"

He smiled and took a sip of coffee. "I came to apologize for earlier today."

"You mean for walking past me and not saying hello at the station? Gee, couldn't that have waited until the sun came up, or not at all? Better yet, a simple phone call?"

"I tried. Went straight to voicemail several times."

I'd forgotten my cell was turned off and made a mental note to pay the bill after I deposited the cash in the bank. "It's not like it was a big deal. I figured you got in some trouble for not arresting me, so no sweat."

"I did, but that's not the reason I ignored you."

"Okay, so spit it out then. I'm freezing."

Cliff glanced up and down the street then lowered his voice. "Like I said, I'm sorry for being rude earlier. It wasn't just because Greenwood had me put on perpetual night shift for the foreseeable future. It's because we exchanged unpleasant words when he forced me to alter my original report."

"I assume you mean the part about me?"

Cliff nodded. A growing sense of unease slithered around in my stomach. Even under the dim light of the moon and street lamp, I noticed Cliff looked upset.

No, not upset.

Worried.

I found the thought sort of funny. After all these years of being a nobody in the town, not a person around to be concerned about my welfare other than Eleanor, suddenly people were interested in my pathetic life.

"Okay, Cliff. I'm tired and like I said, it's freezing out here. Stop being so cryptic and just say what you came to so I can go back to bed. I've got a big day ahead of me, and I'm not exactly a ball of sunshine when I don't get a good night's rest."

Cliff's eyes narrowed into small slits. "I heard. Starting a new job tomorrow, or I mean, today. Don't you find that odd?"

"Eleanor said the rumor mill in this town was fast. She was way off. Apparently, news travels now at warp speed." Cliff huffed, clearly irritated at my response, so I added, "Yes, I do find it odd, but how does any of this concern you? Why do you care?"

"Are you serious?"

"About what?"

"Look, Renee. I know I've been gone for a long time. Been back here less than a year and return to discover this town ain't changed one bit. Ridgeport's still run by the same pompous, self-centered blowhards who have their own agendas. I care because asking a cop to alter a report and remove a key component is wrong, not to mention illegal. You didn't find some random stranger floating in the lake. You found the Mayor's wife for God sakes! Every single T should be crossed and I dotted. Nothing left hidden or overlooked, especially now that it looks like Mrs. Cayhill was murdered and not a jumper.

Something major is wrong when that doesn't happen. Major."

"Cliff, I didn't ask for any of this! Jesus! I go out to the lake for some peace and quiet and find myself in the middle of a nightmare! Like I don't already have a plateful of garbage in my life! Though I had nothing to do with the decision, I'm glad I don't have to deal with it anymore. The investigation—it's not my problem. What I don't get is why are you talking to me about it? If you're so worried, shouldn't you voice your thoughts to the Sheriff or something?"

Cliff set the coffee mug on the hood and moved closer. Worry had shifted over to fear. Seeing it on his face made me shudder. The Clifton Simpson I remembered from high school was a tough jock, not a worrier.

"I did talk to the Sheriff. H e informed me if I wanted to keep my job I needed to look the other way and follow Detective Greenwood's instructions."

The answer ignited the sense of unease, turning it into a fire pit. My stomach burned. "Oh, brother."

"Renee, please, listen to me. I can tell from your face and body language you agree with me. You know something is wrong. I know they offered you a job and probably the reward money, and somehow, I have a feeling that isn't all they dangled to keep you silent. There's a reason why, and I guarantee you, it isn't a good one. I came by to apologize, but also to tell you I think you might be in danger."

Pulling my robe tighter, I took a step back. "Danger? That's...ridiculous, Cliff. I bumped up against a dead body. I didn't see anyone out there, didn't touch anything, didn't do a damn thing except scream, so what part of that puts me in danger?"

"I don't have an answer just yet, only a gut feeling. My instincts are never wrong, Renee. Never. Listening to them is what kept me alive for years in the military."

I threw my hands up in defeat. "Okay, you win. I'm officially freaked out. Thanks, Cliff. Thanks for stopping by and ruining the beginning of what could have been a new, happy life for me. I should have known better. I don't have that kind of luck!"

Cliff took my hands in his own and pulled me close. His warm breath grazed my cold cheek. "Don't, Renee. I know you've been through hard times. I kept up with you while gone, and I'm so sorry for what you endured."

Another light bulb went off. "You've been spying on me?" The look of shame on Cliff's face answered my question. I backed up, yanking my hands from his grip. "No one called in a report about a woman alone at the lake, did they? You followed me out there!"

Closing the space between us, Cliff reached out and grabbed my hands again. "I did, but only because I've been trying to figure out a way to approach you. I wanted to reconnect again. I knew you moved in with Eleanor after losing your job. I saw you leave the house, so I followed, hoping I'd catch you out at the store or something. When I realized you were heading to the lake, I knew something was wrong. No one goes out there unless they're ready to end it all. That's what you planned to do, isn't it?"

A lump of angry tears formed in my throat. Rather than respond, I kept my thoughts to myself and stared at the ground. Humiliation and shame washed over me, along with a heavy dose of irritation my stupid, spur-of-the-moment thoughts about ending my life had been discovered by someone else.

Pulling me closer, Cliff whispered, "Thought so. Renee, you aren't alone in this world. Many people would be devastated if you finished what you started out there. Me most of all."

Finding the courage to look Cliff in the eyes, I raised my head, surprised to find a few tears trickling down his face. They made my own flow.

"I'm not an asshole who decided to come over here and dump more stress on your shoulders. I'm here because my instincts told me I needed to protect you. I care because, well, I always have. Ever since our first kiss."

Cliff's voice—the words spoken in soft,

hushed tones—lulled me into a trance. I'd only kissed two men in my entire life: Cliff and Billy. Out of the duo, only bedded one. I had never experienced the rush of warmth and safety Cliff's words had on me.

And I didn't like it one bit.

"I don't need protection—"

My plea was squashed by a set of full, warms lips. The kiss was gentle, soft, and yet full of hunger and passion. It took me back thirty-three years to the first time Cliff's mouth descended on mine in high school. The physical connection with another person left me breathless and hungry for more.

So of course, I pulled away.

"Like I said, I don't need protection."

Eyes full of unreadable emotions, Cliff touched his finger to my chin and tilted my head toward his. "Yes, Renee, you do. Not only from yourself but others. I promise I'll stay a safe distance and keep an eye on you like I've been doing since I came back. I'll let you seek me out when you're ready for all of me. Just know I'm here. Waiting."

Before I could say another word, Cliff was inside his patrol car. He turned around in Eleanor's driveway and drove away, leaving me standing at the edge of the road, stunned.

I trudged back inside, wondering if I was really awake or still dreaming.

At least, if it was a dream, it was a sexy, suspenseful one.

Chapter Seven

"YOU SLEEP OKAY?"

Eleanor poured another cup of coffee and joined me at the kitchen table. I wondered if she heard me get up earlier. I didn't want to start a new day on the wrong foot since our little emotional connection the night before, so I danced around the truth.

"Not really. Woke up from a nightmare about my dad. Went outside to get some fresh air to clear my head."

"Bet it was awkward to be outside in your pajamas and a robe when Cliff Simpson drove up."

God, the woman missed *nothing*! Did she ever sleep? I couldn't wait to move back home so every move I made wasn't witnessed by Eleanor's all-seeing eyes.

"Not as awkward as this conversation, Eleanor," I laughed. Deciding to broach the subject first, I added, "I assume you saw him kiss me, too?"

Expecting a snarky response, or at least, a disapproving glance, Eleanor shocked me when she grinned.

"I did. That boy's been sweet on you ever since high school. Sure took him long enough to come courting."

Groaning on the inside, I wondered if Eleanor had seen our first kiss in the parking lot of the school as well. Since she had been a teacher at Ridgeport High, the probability was in her favor.

"High school crushes don't last, Eleanor."

The minute I said the words, I felt like

an ass. A shadow of pain crossed Eleanor's face. Though the comment had nothing to with Billy, I doubted she would believe me if I tried to clarify the statement.

"Some do. Why do you think he left Ridgeport after he graduated? You weren't on the market any longer."

My mouth fell open. "That's...no, that's just silly. Cliff enlisted in the army and got away from this hellhole we call home. End of story. Had nothing to do with me."

Eleanor stood and headed to the living room. Over her shoulder, she casually commented, "You're a strong woman, Renee, but sometimes, blind as a newborn kitten. About a lot of things. Have a good first day at work. Keep your eyes on Mayor Cayhill. You still going in at ten?"

"Yes. He wanted to give me a chance to handle a few personal things before I started. You know, like taking the hush money to the mortgage company, paying my cell bill. Exciting stuff."

Eleanor yelled from the living room,

"Like I said, Renee, just watch yourself. Cliff and I can only do so much."

Chuckling to myself, I finished the rest of my breakfast in silence, marveling at how life had changed in a matter of days.

"GOOD MORNING. I need to see the manager."

The young woman behind the counter at First Arkansas Loan tried to look interested at the customer in front of her. It didn't work. A hint of irritation floated behind her big eyes.

"He's not available. May I help you with something?"

Glancing at my watch, I grimaced. It was fifteen after nine and I still had to stop by the cell store before heading to my new job. Figuring cash would interest lil Miss Fussy Pants, I pulled out the wad of cash from my purse. I counted out six-thousand dollars and slid the crisp bills across the counter.

"You may. I need to apply this money to the mortgage you have on my house and get it out of foreclosure."

"I'll need to get the manager."

I smiled, feeling a sense of triumph at knocking the smugness from the teller's face. "Yes, I know. That's why I asked for him to begin with."

AT NINE-FIFTY, I pulled into the back parking lot of City Hall, foreclosure averted and cell phone functioning once again. Despite all the craziness of the last three days, the dire warnings from Eleanor and Cliff, and the constant pain in my back, I was happy.

Maybe happy wasn't the best word. Relieved—yes, that was the one.

And nervous. I'd been out of work for

almost nine months, and I had no idea what type of office work I'd be doing.

Shutting the car off, I stared at my outfit. Boring, black slacks and a button-up white shirt I'd bought at Walmart over three years ago. A weird sheen on the pants from where the material had thinned made me cringe.

"Okay, stop it. I can buy new clothes tomorrow. Maybe make an appointment and get my hair colored, too. City employees don't work on Saturdays. Quit worrying about what others think! It's not like people around here don't already know I'm poor!"

Pulling my gaze away from my bland wardrobe, I scanned the parking lot. Only a few cars sat in designated spaces. Ridgeport City Hall loomed in front of me. It was an impressive site even though it was the oldest building in the county. Though a smaller version, the design was meant to mimic the State Capitol in Little Rock.

Summoning up the courage to get out of the car, I grabbed my purse and trudged inside, wondering what sort of new, crazy adventure awaited me through the massive oak doors.

Hopefully, my first day at work would be boring as Hell. I certainly didn't need any more excitement. I chuckled to myself, remembering how only three days ago, I sat at the edge of the lake and wanted some movie magic—some Hollywood sparkle—in my life.

"Better make sure to be careful what I wish for," I muttered while opening the door.

"SO, HOW WAS IT?"

I stopped at the entrance to the kitchen and gawked at the table. Eleanor had outdone herself. She'd set out her fine china and silverware, along with a white linen tablecloth covering the ancient dining room table. In the middle of the display sat a fresh vase of flowers and two candles. Though the serving dishes were covered, judging by the smells wafting from the kitchen, she'd fixed something Italian.

Eleanor hadn't fixed an Italian meal since Kyle passed away. Though she was an amazing cook, and her spaghetti with homemade marinara sauce legendary, she refused to make any sort of pasta dish. Knowing she fixed it for me—and how doing so probably brought back sad memories—made tears well up in my eyes.

"Boring compared to this surprise! Wow, Eleanor, I don't know what to say. You certainly didn't need to go all this trouble for me."

Motioning for me to sit, Eleanor moved to the other side of the table. "Hush, girl. Eat. The way I figured, y our d ay w ould be horrible or exciting. A good, warm meal would make things either better if the day stunk, or a fantastic way to celebrate a good one. Besides, it's probably the last time I'll cook for two again anytime soon since I assume you'll be moving back home."

Sitting down across from her, I smiled.

"It smells heavenly and I know it'll taste even better. Again, thank you."

Eleanor took my plate and loaded it with enough spaghetti and garlic bread to feed three people. "Tell me about your day. Did Mayor Cayhill say anything to you?"

"Actually, I didn't even see him today. I spent most of my time in the file room with Traci Rogers. She's in charge of training me. Wow, the amount of paper filling those drawers could probably circle the globe twice. In this digital age, it seems like a waste of trees to me."

"Traci Rogers? She any kin to Sylvia Rogers?" Eleanor asked while handing me the plate.

Taking a huge bite, I nodded. "Yes. Sylvia's her aunt. You know, I haven't seen Traci in years. She mentioned she moved back here last year from Russellville. Divorce."

"Seems like no one stays in it for the long haul anymore."

Unwilling to comment on the baited

statement, I shoved another mouthful of pasta into my mouth.

"Did you get your mortgage all straightened out?"

"Yep. Oh, and my phone's working again. God, I dread stepping foot in my house. I can't image how dirty it is. Probably has dust bunnies the size of small dogs. If you don't mind, I planned on staying with you through the weekend. It'll give me time to go over there and clean up before I grab what little I had left from your garage and settle back in. Is that okay?"

"Of course."

"Oh, and I bought some hair color, too. Would you mind helping me cover this gray after we eat? I'll probably need help with the back."

"Sure, though I don't understand why you don't just go get it done at Myrna's Salon. She'll do a much better job."

I sighed. "I'm trying to be frugal with the money, Eleanor. No telling how long I'll have this job."

Eleanor smiled. "Such a smart girl.

Listen, I'm glad you're waiting until next weekend to move back so I can help."

"No need for you to do that, Eleanor. I can manage."

"I didn't say you couldn't. I said I wanted to help and that I wouldn't be available this weekend."

Pausing in mid-chew, it dawned on me why she wouldn't be around tomorrow.

Visiting day.

The last Saturday of each month, Eleanor made the fifty-mile trek down to the Varner Unit in Pine Bluff. She'd never asked me outright to accompany her though she did hint from time to time how difficult the drive was at her age.

After a visit with her vile offspring, Eleanor wouldn't answer the phone, talk, or even eat all day on Sunday. Instead, she'd shut herself in her bedroom until Monday morning. Before I'd moved in, I didn't realize how hard the visits with Billy were on her. After experiencing her reaction in person last month, I knew.

They devastated her. Physically and

emotionally drained her of all joy, happiness, and pep. When I watched her emerge from the bedroom last time, it seemed the woman aged five years.

Unsure what to say, I continued to eat. Thankfully, I was saved from having to come up with some type of stupid response when my phone rang. "Excuse me, Eleanor."

Though my back throbbed from standing so much earlier, I practically jumped out of the chair. By the fourth ring, I made it to the living room and snatched the phone from my purse.

The number was local but I didn't recognize it. Considering the way things had gone in my life the last few days, it could be anyone.

"Hello?"

"Hey, Renee. Did I interrupt your dinner? I can call back later if I did."

"Cliff?"

"Yes, ma'am. You busy?"

Turning away so Eleanor couldn't see me from the dining room, I moved to the window and lowered my voice. "Actually, I am in the middle of dinner with Eleanor."

"Sorry. I only called to offer up my arms to assist you tomorrow. You know, with moving?"

"Good Lord!" I huffed, "How did you...oh, never mind. Small town equals fast news. I remember now. The gossip lines surpass a high-speed internet connection. I, uh, wasn't planning on moving stuff just yet. It's been two months since I've been there, so I was going to give it a good cleaning first."

"Well, that settles it. I'm a great housekeeper. Cleanliness is one of the many things burned into my brain from the army. What time shall I meet you?"

I hesitated before answering. Part of me wanted Cliff to be there so I could pick his brain a little about the investigation. Another part wanted him there so maybe another sweet, stolen kiss would happen. Unfortunately, those two parts were trumped by the long-standing, Billy Runsford-inspired edict of remaining alone.

While standing in the living room of the

house the man used to live in, his mother sitting in the next room, a wave of anger hit me. The anger wasn't at Eleanor, or even at Billy.

It was all directed internally.

There, I'd said his name again *without* having an anxiety attack.

Something stopped me from killing myself, and it wasn't just Martha Cayhill's bloated corpse. Would I have actually gone through with it? After all, I'd stopped at three pills. Another something pushed me to stand up to Gretchen rather than slink away like a coward. Yet another something gave me the confidence to get out of bed and start a new job, all the while knowing something about the entire offer stunk to high Heaven.

Those somethings all stemmed from only one source.

Determination.

I let the anger take control for a minute. No, I wouldn't hide any longer. Wouldn't shield myself from life because I'd been too freaking scared to live it. Not anymore.

It was time to make changes in my little

world. The first one would start with Clifton Simpson. His lips, those strong arms, God, I wanted to feel them both again. To bask in his strength, revel in the rush from touching his skin.

Oh, perhaps my cynical view of the world was changing!

"Renee? You still there?"

Puffing out my chest with a lungful of air, I let it out in controlled bursts. "Yes, Cliff, I am. You said you're working permanent nights, right? Shift ends at seven a.m.?"

Cliff chuckled. "Yep."

"Then how about one or so? Will that give you enough time to catch some sleep before I put you to work?"

"Perfect. Looking forward to seeing you tomorrow, Renee. Enjoy the rest of your dinner."

Disconnecting the call, a wide grin formed.

The phone call was the first time since I was sixteen I'd ever flirted with anyone, and judging by the seductive, sexy tone in Cliff's voice, I'd succeeded at it.

Yay me!

Turning my phone to silent, I put it back in my purse and rejoined Eleanor.

"Sorry about that. So, after I get my house back in order tomorrow, I'd like to reciprocate and cook you a lovely dinner. Of course, it won't be near as tasty as this, but I'll try."

Eleanor's green eyes glinted with mischief. "What a nice idea. Will Cliff be joining us as well?"

Chuckling, I shook my head. "No, Eleanor. Just me and you. Tomorrow's going to take a lot out of us both for different reasons, so it'll be our version of Ladies' Night In. Okay?"

Rather than responding, Eleanor smiled and set about the business of cleaning up dinner.

We were making progress, and that was a good thing.

A good thing, indeed.

"Come on, let's go wash those grays away. You want to look your best for your new suitor, right?"

With a half-hearted groan, I rose from the chair and helped with the dishes, wondering what kind of probing questions Eleanor would ask while coloring my hair.

8

MONDAY CAME AND went in a whirlwind, my second full day at work a blur of paper and more instructions. Traci was patient and helpful while showing me how to scan and save documents to the main server, navigate through the various computer programs, and get into the swing of the ways at the office. Since I'd never worked in one before, the only real skill I had was answering the multi-line phone system. It was the same kind I'd used at the call center, so at least, I wasn't a total dud.

By the time four-thirty rolled around, I wanted to scream. My back throbbed in agony. Unaccustomed to being on my feet so much, even wearing flats didn't help. Of course, all the hours Cliff and I spent cleaning my house on Saturday didn't help, either. When Traci shut down the computers for the night, I was raring to leave and soak in a hot bath.

"Have a great evening, Renee. And stop worrying—you're catching on just fine, just like Mayor Cayhill said you would. Of course, I knew you would the minute I heard you were coming on board. You were smart as a whip in high school."

Thankful the other two office workers had already left, I decided it was safe to pick Traci's brain. "Thank you. Nice to hear a compliment now and again. My last supervisor certainly didn't understand the concept. Your memories of days long since passed certainly don't match up with mine. I seem to remember you had to help me with Algebra."

Traci laughed. "God, I forgot all about that! Ugh, what was our teacher's name? Mrs. Parnell?"

"Yep. Poopy Parnell is what I believe you used to call her."

"That's right! The woman had the worst breath ever! Hence my choice of the nickname."

Shifting gears, I steered the conversation back to the mayor. "I hope Mayor Cayhill agrees with your assessment when he comes back to work. He's going through so much right now I don't want to add any more stress thinking he hired a useless employee."

We stepped outside and Traci locked the doors. The rush of cold air sent pangs of pain down my lower back. I wondered how long I'd last before having to admit I did need surgery. Maybe I could keep the job long enough with the city to qualify for insurance benefits and get my discs fixed before the Mayor decided to let me go.

Somehow, I sensed the job wouldn't be permanent.

"Well don't you worry, you won't. Gosh, we've all been so concerned about him. I mean, the man about lost his mind when Martha disappeared. He never gave up searching for her. Told me he spent thousands of dollars on some big shot private investigator out of Little Rock and look what it got him: squat. Poor man honestly believed she'd simply gone off her medication and wandered away. After all this time, she turns up—dead—at the lake, not even ten miles from their house. Tragic."

"Very. I can't imagine how hard this is on him. I guess he'll come back to work when he has a chance to digest it all. I mean, it's one thing to come to grips with her passing but a whole new bag of pain got thrown into the mix when murder was added in."

Traci stopped at her car and grimaced. "Lord, I just can't figure it out! Who in the world would want to harm Martha? The woman was practically a saint."

"Well, hopefully, the cops will figure out

who did it soon. With all the new things technology and forensic science can do, it shouldn't take too long."

"I hope not. Jeez, I move back here thinking I'd spend the remainder of my days in a safe place, away from all the craziness and crime of a big city. Silly me."

"Cruelty and ugliness aren't limited to a big area. Anywhere people live, no matter how small the town, bad things happen. It's called human nature."

Traci looked at me, sadness beaming from her big, blue eyes. "I know, it's just...well, you'd think in such a close-knit community, people would watch out for each other. That's how I recalled my youth when in Russellville. When I divorced my husband, that's why I didn't even flinch about moving back. Now, after what's happened, I'm beginning to wonder if I should reconsider and move to Little Rock. At least I'd be closer to my kids."

"Don't worry, Traci. Like I said, the cops will nail whoever did this and we'll all be able to put this nightmare behind us. Get back to living our quiet, normal lives."

Traci nodded then grimaced, pointing at my car. "Uh-oh. Looks like you got a parking ticket."

Turning, I followed her gaze. A small, white piece of paper was stuck under the windshield wiper of my car. Great. A ticket. Seriously? Hadn't the rumor mill informed everyone I now worked for the city?

Forcing my legs to move, I stepped over and yanked it off.

"Don't worry, Renee. We'll get Mayor Cayhill to fix i t f or y ou. H e's g ood about things like that."

Wow, she had no idea how true those words really were. Peyton Cayhill was the King of Fix Things the Way I Want Them.

The envelope didn't contain a ticket. It was a handwritten note from Cliff. Heat flushed my face despite the cold.

Traci unlocked her car and opened the door. "Say, Renee? How about we go have dinner and catch up? Rehashing thirty years of memories might take a big batch of chips and a few margaritas."

Stuffing the note into my purse, back still on fire, I stared at Traci's eager face. If she drank enough tequila to loosen her tongue, I might be able to pry out more information. Though we were the same age, the years had been more than kind to the woman. She didn't look a day over thirty-five, so of course, that miffed me.

Oh, God—my mother just left the grave and jumped right into my head.

Despite the fact my back disagreed, I pushed the pain away. The last time I'd spent an evening out with a girlfriend was with Gretchen, and that was over eight years prior.

New life; new man; new trajectory. Why the hell not?

"Sure, that sounds great. How about La Hacienda? They've got the best food. And tequila. Lots and lots of tequila. I'll follow you."

"Oh, fun! Girl time! Just what I needed. Actually, what I think we both do. My treat."

"I'll meet you there."

Traci squealed and jumped into her car. In seconds, she disappeared from the parking lot. I started up my car, and while waiting for the heater to blow out warm air rather than frigid, decided to see what Cliff's note said.

"Hello, gorgeous. Hope your first Monday was a good one. Saturday was one of the best days I've had in a long time. Did I mention how much I loved the new hair? If not, I do. Sexy, sexy, sexy! Even cleaning is a joy when around you. Thank you for letting me help—I know letting others into your world is hard. Working tonight, but I'm off tomorrow. I'd love to make you dinner. Hamburgers with pickles, no onion, and mustard and ketchup on top, right? Call me if you want a gourmet meal prepared by thankful hands."

How in the world did Cliff remember the way I liked my hamburgers? The man had the memory of an elephant.

My stomach did a little flip-flop when I let my thoughts wander about what other body parts resembled others in the animal kingdom.

Pulling out my phone, I sent him a quick text:

"*I enjoyed watching your muscles ripple under the thin t-shirt you wore. Assume that was done on purpose? Trying to bait me with your brawn? Ha! And yes, I do believe you commented on my new look. Thanks. Since I know you're watching my every move, I'm heading to dinner with Traci at La Hacienda. Hoping to score some good intel. You coming by tonight? It's gonna be cold, so I'll have the coffee hot and ready.*"

Setting my phone in the passenger seat, I left the parking lot. I barely made it to the highway when my phone beeped with a response. A tingle of warmth spread through my groin and I had to force myself to wait to see what Cliff sent until I pulled into the parking lot of La Hacienda.

"*Just thinking about seeing you again heats me up. I hope coffee is code for something else.*"

Oh, it was.

For sure, though certainly no more than a kiss until I moved out of Eleanor's. The thought of her catching us in a compromising position made me cringe.

139

Plus, I hadn't had sex in so long, I wasn't sure my vagina would cooperate. The space between my legs was probably drier than the Sahara.

Wow, I'd certainly given up on life *way* too soon.

Exiting the car, I made a quick phone call to Eleanor, letting her know I'd be late coming home.

Because it seemed I had a life now—what a foreign concept!

TWO HOURS AND three margaritas later, my back wasn't as tight and my mind pleasantly buzzed. I let Traci take the lead of the topics discussed, figuring it would seem rather obvious if I immediately started our visit by asking probing questions about the Mayor.

Most of our conversation centered on about the demise of her marriage, her twin daughters in their second year of college at UALR, and Edward, Traci's ex-husband. The wound to Traci's heart was still fresh after discovering Edward in bed with one of his students—Traci's bed, mind you!—so I let her vent.

And vent she did, tongue freed to speak her mind after downing five margaritas.

When Traci broached the subject of what my life had been like after she moved away to college, I glossed over the highlights. For the most part, Traci sat across from me, eyes wide with shock and sadness. I didn't delve too deeply because I didn't want to talk about my life.

I came to dinner to dig for some information, and it was time to do so before I drank too much and forgot my questions.

Traci raised the margarita glass for a toast. "Here's to being rid of the pieces of shit in our lives. May they both contract the worst diseases alive and dick's fall off!"

"Shhh, Traci!" I whispered and laughed at the same time. "God, I'd forgotten how funny you are—and loud!"

"Like I give a rat's ass what people around here think," Traci muttered.

She took a long drink and motioned to the waiter for another.

"I really don't either, I just didn't want to call attention to our conversation."

"Why? Afraid some stupid redneck might hear us talk about our collective disgust at those with dicks?"

Traci was thoroughly trashed. I made a mental note to follow her home. Setting down my drink, I leaned forward and whispered, "Because this town has ears everywhere, listening, and I wanted to talk about our boss in private."

Traci's curiosity was piqued. She raised an inquisitive brow. "Oh, local gossip. Goody!"

"No, nothing like that. I don't know anything other than what's been reported on the news. I'm just...worried about my job. With all the stress in his life, and the fact he hasn't been at work the last two days, what if the Mayor has a heart attack—or worse—and I find myself looking for work again?"

"Pft! That's a silly worry, girl! Even when he leaves, the new mayor will leave the current staff in place. That's what he told me when I asked."

"Leave? Mayor Cayhill is leaving?" I gasped.

"Ooops. I'm not supposed to tell anyone. Damn! I'm the one full of gossip, not you! Must admit it sort of feels good to finally let it out. I've been keeping the secret for weeks now. Guess it's okay to tell you since you work with us now. Promise me you'll keep it to yourself until he announces it next week?"

"Of course. What's spoken at the table, stays at the table."

Traci let out a huff of air. "Thank you! Shit, I guess Edward was right—I'm a lousy drunk. Talk too much."

"Screw Edward and what he thinks or thought about you! As employees, we have a right to know if our jobs are in jeopardy, right?"

"You're right! Listen, don't worry. The guard will change soon once the final signatures are completed and filed. There's big things happening in our little town. Big changes, and I for one can't wait, though I will miss working for Mayor Cayhill. It'll be strange to call him Judge Cayhill. I hope Mayor Greenwood will be as easy to work for."

I choked on a chip and nearly coughed myself to death. After recovering, I blurted out, "Judge Cayhill? I didn't know he was a lawyer?"

"He's not, but that's what they call the County Judge around here, remember?"

"Cayill's taking over as County Judge? Why? When did the current one decide to leave?"

"He's got prostate cancer. Stepping down next week. Poor man."

Mind spinning at all the crazy news, I took another drink of water to clear my throat. The other juicy tidbit she tossed needed clarification. " Greenwood? A s in current Detective Greenwood? He's going to be our new Mayor?"

"Yep. You know him? I just met him the

other day, and he seems okay. Sort of quiet and reserved, but okay."

I took a few more sips of water, unwilling to drink any more alcohol. My head was spinning from the shocking news and didn't need to add to it. "I've met him once or twice. Small town, you know."

"One still full of old-school back rubbing."

Pausing to collect my thoughts and let the waiter step away after bringing Traci another round, I let the news soak in. My plan to extract some information had taken a really dark turn. I didn't like any of the revelations.

Not at all.

"So the mayor will move over to Whitten County as the new judge, and Richard Greenwood will step up as mayor. Are you sure? How's that even possible without holding an election or something?"

Traci laughed. "Girl, you've lived in this town your whole life. You know how the political game is played. Scratch my back, I'll scratch yours."

"That is true, but still doesn't explain how they'll get around letting people vote."

"Election season ain't until next November. They're using some archaic law put on the books back when Noah was a baby. When I was cleaning out a jam in the copier last week, I found a piece of paper stuck inside. It was a copy of Order 16, dated back from the 1930s. Said something about what happens when a sitting County Judge becomes ill or unable to perform his duties, he can appoint anyone of his choosing to replace him until the next election."

"Okay, that explains one thing, but not about appointing a new mayor."

"Wrong. The Order applies to all county and city employees. Back when it was written, the two entities weren't separated."

"So, they're announcing all this next week?"

"Yes. They need to hurry and transfer power before the current judge passes away. He's in Stage 4. Plus, if the documents aren't signed by next Friday, the land deal's off."

"Land deal? What land deal?"

Traci grinned, clearly enjoying the chance to release all the secrets she'd kept bottled up. She motioned for me to move closer after glancing around to ensure no one was listening. "Bradford Lake. Some out-of-state investors want to buy it, drain it, and convert it into an automotive parts manufacturing plant. It'll bring a ton of revenue into the county. That's why Mayor Cayhill ain't been at work. He's been in meetings with a slew of lawyers hammering out the details. When his wife's body turned up there, it almost shut the negotiations down."

I damn near fainted.

Not just because of the shocking turn of events, or how hearing them tied everything together. Stunned into silence, old childhood memories and pain swarmed inside my mind.

Dad.

Cyndi.

The bike.

Oh, shit. The family secret I'd kept inside

me for so long—if it were actually true—would be revealed.

All the years I'd searched for my father, I'd found nothing. No work history. No activity on his Social Security Number. No child support, no birthday or Christmas cards. My mother's drunken confession.

If Bradford Lake was scheduled to be drained, my worst fears would be unearthed. The room started to spin.

"Renee? You okay?"

Shaking my head, I covered my mouth and mumbled, "Gonna be sick," then ran to the bathroom.

9

I HEARD TRACI come inside the restroom, turn the sink on and then grab a bunch of paper towels.

"You okay?"

I flushed the toilet and exited the stall, stumbling my way to the sink. "Yeah. Obviously, I can't hold my liquor. Haven't drunk this much in years. The last time I did, I wound up pregnant."

Traci giggled. "Don't worry. I certainly can't knock you up."

I gave her a weak smile. "True."

"I've had way more and I'm fine. Well, I mean, I don't feel sick or anything. You should've eaten more food. Then again, maybe I should've kept my mouth shut and not freaked you out."

Taking the damp towels, I wiped my face and turned on the faucet. After rinsing my mouth and spitting, I said, "Stop. My worshiping the porcelain throne had nothing to do with what you told me though it is shocking. It's just been a really long last seven days and I overindulged."

Traci slumped against the counter and yanked the clip from her head. Mounds of thick, sable hair spilled around her shoulders. Even when trashed, she was still beautiful. I didn't dare look at my own reflection, afraid I'd puke again.

"Wow, think I stood too fast. Got the spins."

"Why don't you let me drive you home? I feel fine now that I yakked up all the tequila."

The door opened before Traci had a chance to respond. The night was just full of surprises.

"Oh, this brings me back to high school. Renee and Traci trashed in the bathroom, desperately trying to clean themselves up so others won't notice."

I wanted to crawl back into the stall. The last person I needed to see was Gretchen Chase, yet there she stood, face full of righteous condemnation.

Traci snorted, "Well, hello to you too, Gretchen. Your face has changed but your mouth sure hasn't."

Okay, that was funny so of course I laughed.

Gretchen walked to the mirror and opened her purse. While applying more gloss to lips already coated with way too much, she gave me a smirk then said, "Only back in town a short time and already picked up bad habits again, Traci? Hmmm, must be the company you keep. Didn't your momma warn you about hanging out with white trash?"

That did it. I threw the wet paper towels on the counter, ready to give my former friend an earful. She only thought what I'd said to her at Walmart was bad.

Traci beat me to the punch. "She did, which is why I never came knocking on your door to say I was back."

"Oh, what a witty comeback! Guess you aren't as drunk as you look. And smell."

"You just proved your mother didn't teach you any manners, Gretchen. And this is nothing like high school. Back then, you were just as trashed and not a bitch."

Traci burst out laughing and headed toward the door. Gretchen's face was red again and anger burned behind her eyes. Gracing her with a smirk of my own, I turned and followed Traci.

"Watch your back, Traci. Like I said, Renee hasn't changed since high school. She's still the same weird, lost soul constantly in need of validation. She'll pull you into the pity-party known as her life and try to drown you, too. My advice is to walk away before you get sucked in."

"I suppose my other option is to walk down the road you did and abandon a friend in need? No thanks, Gretchen. There's only room in this small town for one hateful twat."

Traci yanked the door open and we stumbled out into the dining area, laughing hysterically. Several patrons turned and looked our way and neither of us cared. Throwing a wad of cash on the table, Traci muttered something I didn't catch and staggered toward the front door.

The moon was bright and the air frigid while we walked. Traci fumbled for her keys, giggling like a teenager while continuing to spew out hateful things about Gretchen Chase. Though I sort of enjoyed listening to her verbally shred Gretchen, I also knew she was way too intoxicated to drive.

Reaching for her keys, I said, "Traci, let me take you home."

"I'm fine! Besides, if I leave my car here, how will I get to work in the morning?"

"I'll stop by and pick you up on my way in."

Figuring I was in for an argument, I was pleasantly surprised when Traci dropped the keys back inside her purse. "Okay. Just no talking loud in the morning because I have a feeling my head will be pounding."

I looked over at my piece of junk and then back to Traci's nice SUV. If I was a car thief, I know which one I'd pick. "Let's take your vehicle and leave mine. Chances of someone stealing it are nil. I promise I won't go anywhere except your place and then back to mine. Okay?"

By now, Traci was leaning against the passenger door of the Lincoln Navigator, her eyes half-closed. "Whatever you say, driver."

After helping cram Traci's drunk ass into the passenger seat, I climbed behind the wheel and started the engine. I'd never been inside a vehicle with heated, leather seats, or seen one with so many buttons and lights.

"I guess I need to ask you where you live, huh?" I muttered while fiddling w ith the confusing buttons to find t he o ne t o move the seat closer. Traci was a good four inches taller than me and my feet barely reached the pedals.

"Ha, that would probably help! You remember where my aunt lives off of Highway 9, right?"

My heart skipped two beats. I remembered. Of course, she lived less than two miles from Suicide Lake. God, I couldn't escape the water no matter how hard I tried. Mental images of the muddy bottom with two skeletons stuck in the muck next to a rotting Harley made my stomach queasy again. I forced myself not to puke. "Um, yeah. Been a long time, but I think so. Are you staying with Sylvia?"

Traci exploded into a pile of snorts and giggles while I backed out of the parking lot and turned left onto the main highway. "Hell no! She may be kin, but we aren't exactly close. I'm staying at the rental cabin on her property until I save up enough cash to buy a house. College tuition for two is expensive, even though Edward is paying half. The old bitch surprised me when she called and offered to let me stay there rent-free. That's why I didn't move to Little Rock."

"That was nice of her. At least you aren't living with Sylvia."

Traci shifted in the seat and stared at me. "Oh, sorry. That was rude of me. I'd forgotten about your situation. I can't imagine how hard it's been."

"At first, it was, that's for sure. The time we've spent in close proximity to one another has, um, opened up a new door in our relationship. Eleanor's been through some tough times and so have I. Guess living together forced us to wear each other's shoes for a while. We learned a lot about each other."

"That's so nice, but still creepy if you ask me. I mean, the history between you two! Does she ever talk about it?"

"No. Not really. Sometimes she hints around it but never comes out and directly mentions Billy's name."

"Well, I admire you both for different reasons. She is a strong woman and obviously a kind soul to offer her place up to you. You've got to be one tough chick mentally to withstand living with the mother of your ex, especially considering where he is at the moment."

"Eleanor is a kind soul for sure. In terms of me? Well, let's just say this job was a Godsend. I'm moving back home this weekend and will enjoy more than I can express the joy of living alone."

We chatted a few more minutes about trivial things while I navigated the dark, twisty roads leading to the bowels of Whitten County. I cringed when we passed the road leading to Bradford Lake, and a lump of tears formed while passing the entrance to Ten Mile Cemetery less than a mile later.

When Traci pointed to the correct road on the left, I turned on the blinker and glanced in the rear-view mirror out of habit. A twinge of fear made the hairs stand on my neck when the faint glimmer of headlights in the distance appeared.

Ignoring the stupid paranoia, I dropped Traci off, helped her inside the cabin, and then limped my way back to the SUV. The buzz was long gone and my back throbbed.

Once back on Highway 9, I zoned out, thinking about all the little bombshells Traci dropped during dinner. Though a bit painful, I didn't really care about the dramatic little episode in the bathroom with Gretchen. The interaction paled in comparison to the revelations revealed from Traci's drunken words.

My world was on the cusp of crumbling around me. If what Traci said was true, then Mom's dirty little secret would be revealed, giving Gretchen Chase, and everyone else in Whitten County, something to gossip about for years.

I put the SUV in park and stared out the windshield. Without consciously realizing it, I'd turned down the road leading to Ten Mile Cemetery. The headlights illuminated rows and rows of headstones in front of me.

I didn't care about the pain in my back as I climbed out of the seat and walked across the dry grass. Memorized from years of making the pilgrimage numerous times, I stopped in front of the small markers where the bodies of my mother and son rested six-feet under my feet.

William Bracy Runsford – *beloved son* and *Caroline Clark Thornton* – *mother*. The etched words on the marble headstones had faded over time. The ache inside my chest for William pounded. I hated myself for thinking I was almost glad he'd died, because if my son had lived, his life would be shattered soon when Suicide Lake gave up her secrets.

Lowering myself to the cold ground, I ran my fingers over the words, wishing there was a third grave next to them. "Oh, Mom, I hope you were lying to me. Dad needs to be right here, next to you, the way things are supposed to be. Why did you tell me? Why did you ruin my life? You shouldn't have told me! I was just a kid for God's sake! I'd rather die thinking Dad left us for another woman than knowing the truth."

The sound of gravel crunching stopped me from collapsing into a blubbering heap on top of Mom's grave. Turning, I shielded my eyes from a bright set of headlights. Great, someone else decides to visit the cemetery.

The lights shut off a nd footsteps approached. The fear from before was back so I stood and headed back to Traci's SUV.

"Renee? What are you doing here?"

Shocked, I stammered, "Cliff? What...are you...did you follow me?"

He moved out of the shadows and right next to me. "I did. You shouldn't be driving."

The tension in Cliff's voice—and the fact he'd followed me—again, pissed me off. "No, Traci shouldn't have been driving, which is why I drove her home. I'm fine, o ther than the fact I'm sort of getting a tad freaked out. I'm not used to being stalked."

"Renee, I'm not stalking you. I told you before, I'm watching to make sure you're safe. Remember? I saw you two leave La Hacienda and wanted to make sure you didn't have an accident. You've been drinking."

"Watching, stalking. Same thing in my book," I said.

Cliff stepped closer, blocking me from getting back in the SUV. "What's wrong? And don't tell me nothing because I can see it in your face. Talk to me."

There was no way I'd share what was going on with Cliff. He'd find out soon enough anyway. Before we moved any further in our little relationship-dance, it was time to end the music and walk away. "Nothing to talk about, Cliff. I dropped Traci off, stopped by the graves of my loved once since I was out this way, and now I'm heading to Eleanor's. End of story, and end of us. I don't like having my every move monitored. I get enough of that from Eleanor."

Cliff reached out and touched my cheek. His hand was warm and sent shivers of desire pumping through me. "I'm not monitoring every move, Renee. I'm protecting you."

Brushing his hand away, I said, "Again, I don't need your protection. You need to go, Cliff. Find someone else to bother because getting tangled up with me will be your undoing. That's a promise."

Cliff took a step forward and pressed his

body against mine. Even under the dim rays of the moonlight, I could see the raw passion behind his beautiful eyes. "You've been tangled in my heart ever since I was fifteen. I'm not going anywhere."

Before I could protest, Cliff leaned down, cupping my face in his hands. His lips were moist and firm, the kiss more urgent than the one at Eleanor's. I tried to fight the power it had over me, unwilling to let my own passionate thoughts sway me, but the taste of his lips, the power of his hands, overrode my misgivings.

Like two teenagers sneaking out into the woods to neck, Cliff and I sought out each other in the cold, night air. His strong arms held me tight while lips delivered sensual kisses on my mouth and neck. Had the interaction continued any longer, I would have thrown caution to the proverbial wind and let him taste all of me in the backseat of Traci's SUV.

Instead of wallowing around like kids, Cliff pulled away. "See what you do to me,

Renee? Can't keep my head on straight when I'm near you."

Heart racing and blood pounding, I chuckled, "If your plan was to sweep me off my feet and make me forgot what I was saying, it worked. Some moves you've got there, Deputy. Still doesn't change the facts. I don't need protection and—"

"Yes, you do. Your asinine assumptions I'm some freaky stalker and you don't need protection are wrong. I guess while you were at dinner with Traci you didn't hear the latest news?"

Oh, I heard news alright. News that probably turned my hair completely white. Swallowing my fears of what Cliff was about to drop on me, I asked, "News? What news?"

Cliff's attitude shifted from sexual tension to worry. "Martha Cayhill's supposed murderer was arrested an hour ago."

My mouth gaped open, stunned and thrilled the latest local news didn't center on me. "Seriously? Who? And why do you look so worried? This is a good thing, right?"

"If they arrested the real killer it would be. Considering they hauled in ol' Kendrick Paulson, it's not."

The name rang a bell for some reason yet I couldn't place why. "Kendrick Paulson? Why do I know that name?"

"His father, Kendrick Paulson, Sr. The moonshiner."

"Whoa, wait a minute! The guy who killed someone back in the '50s?"

"One and the same. Kendrick, Jr., is just an old hermit living out on his family's property on the other side of Bradford Lake. I saw him when Greenwood brought him in. The man's so frail a puppy would knock him over. No way he killed Martha."

I thought back to what Gretchen said at Walmart and figured t his w as a good opportunity to find out if any of it was true. The news certainly gave me something else to think about besides the impending discovery of my father's bones. "Why do you say that? Is he an invalid or something?"

Cliff s tepped o ver t o h is u nit and retrieved a cup of coffee. T he m an seemed addicted to caffeine. "No, Renee. But he is less than five-six and might weigh all of one-forty when soaking wet. Martha was five-eight and a good ten years younger. She'd put up a fight and probably would have won. Well, at least long enough to get away. Even if I'm wrong about that, I can't picture Kendrick hauling her body from his house to the lake. He ain't strong enough to pick up a sack of grain, much less a body."

Well, there was one tidbit of gossip confirmed. I decided to play dumb. "Wait, are you saying Martha wasn't killed at the lake?"

Cliff raised an eyebrow. "Renee, please. I know you were freaked that night, but surely you didn't miss the fact Martha still had flesh on her, right?"

"Well, yeah, I did notice, but—"

"That's because her body had only been in the lake three days. The rest of the time, she'd been kept in a freezer. One Greenwood discovered in an old barn on Kendrick's property less than four hours ago. Forensics found traces of her blood type inside, and her purse and car keys packed in ice."

Confused, I asked, "If that's the case, why don't you think Kendrick did it? Maybe he had help or something. Maybe a relative?"

"Possible, but what was his motive? According to the autopsy, Martha showed no signs of sexual trauma. No ransom request ever surfaced, so that rules out she was kidnapped for money. Why would Kendrick snatch her, strangle her, tie her up and leave her in his freezer for over fifteen months, then decide to take her out for a dip in the lake? It doesn't add up. None of it."

No, none of it did. The news just muddied the swirling waters of all the other tidbits inside my head. Cold, frightened, and terrified a bout h ow a ll t his w ould e nd, I wanted to go home. I needed to bury my head under the comforter and pretend the entire debacle was nothing more than a product of my vivid nightmares.

"Renee? Did you hear me?" Cliff said, his hands reaching out for my own.

"Oh, uh, sorry. Just shocked about all this, among other things."

Cliff squeezed my hands, bringing one up to his lips for a gentle kiss. "Such as how much I—?"

"Why are you telling me all this?" I interrupted, afraid he was about to say he loved me or something equally disturbing. "Isn't all of this sort of confidential? Aren't you risking your job by talking about it with me or something?"

"Yes, it is, or it will be until he's officially charged. Am I risking my job? Maybe. Do I care? No. You still haven't realized that yet, have you? My only concern is about you."

Looking into Cliff's eyes, the truth dawned on me. He really *did* care, and that was wonderful and heartbreaking at the same time. I'd waited, prayed, hoped, dreamt of being loved, so of course, it happens right before my dirty family secret pops out of the closet.

I summoned every bit of strength I could muster and pulled away. "I'm cold and tired, Cliff. Thanks for watching over me. Really.

But I'll be fine. I c an p rotect m yself. Been doing it for years."

Cliff l ooked w ounded b ut d idn't s ay a word as I climbed back inside the Navigator. When I glanced in the rear-view mirror, he was still in the same spot, staring at the tail lights. Tears rolled down my cheeks as I drove away, wishing my screwed-up life came with a do-over button.

Chapter Ten

"WHO'S VEHICLE IS THAT?"

Eleanor sat perched on the sofa, a cup of hot tea and empty dinner plate resting in her lap. I was glad to see she'd finally eaten something and ventured from her room. Ever since coming back from visiting Billy late Saturday night, she'd been locked inside the bedroom.

Tossing my purse on the kitchen table, I joined her in the living room. "Traci Rogers.

169

She had one-too-many drinks with dinner, so I drove her home."

"That was nice of you. Guess that means your car is still at La Hacienda?"

"Yep. I could leave it parked in downtown Little Rock with the keys inside and doors unlocked and no one would touch it."

Eleanor laughed while gathering the dish. She stood and headed to the kitchen. "Maybe, maybe not. No sense in tempting fate. If someone did decide to steal it, you couldn't afford to buy a new one. Come on, I'll ride with you and we'll go get it."

"Not necessary, Eleanor. I planned on—"

"I insist. Let me change out of my pajamas first."

I knew from the tone in Eleanor's voice it was pointless to argue. God, this night would never end! It was close to nine and I was exhausted, mentally spent, and heartbroken. My brain was overstimulated with too many thoughts and my back was killing me. A hot shower was only steps away but would have to wait another twenty minutes or so.

Eleanor reappeared and we walked in silence outside to Traci's fancy SUV.

Once on the road, Eleanor said, "So, did you hear about Kendrick Paulson?"

I sighed, wondering how Eleanor knew so fast. The ten-o'clock news wasn't on it. Oh, who was I kidding? Eleanor's fingers had always been on the pulse of the town's heartbeat. I considered lying but nixed the idea. Cliff was on the force and Eleanor probably assumed he'd already told me. "Yes."

"From Cliff?"

"Yes."

"Does he think Kendrick did it?"

I glanced over at Eleanor, surprised she had doubts of her own. "Do you?"

Eleanor shook her head. "Nope. Known that man all his life. He may be a strange old codger, but he certainly ain't no killer. Period."

Intrigued by Eleanor's vehement defense, I asked, "What makes you say that, Eleanor? I mean, his father killed someone, so it's possible—"

171

"Just because someone in your family tree killed before don't necessarily mean the trait's tainted the whole root system, Renee."

Ouch. I'd struck a nerve I never intended to hit. The correlation between her and Billy never entered my mind. I needed to learn to think things through better before I opened my mouth. "Okay, bad choice of words. Let me start again. Why do you think Mr. Paulson isn't the killer?"

Eleanor's hackles subsided somewhat as she leaned back in the seat. "Well, for starters, he's an old man who's kept himself hidden most of his life because of his embarrassment over what his dad done so long ago. Two, Kendrick ain't the sharpest tool in the shed, and three, what little brain cells remaining got them a case of dementia."

"How do you know that, Eleanor?"

"Just because I don't talk about things doesn't mean I'm not aware of what goes on where I live. Always felt sorry for poor Kendrick. Kyle did, too. Once a month, we'd fix him a nice basket of helpful items and take them to him. After Kyle passed on, I

172

continued the tradition. Every last Saturday of the month, rain or shine."

"You...do you go before you head to Pine Bluff?" I whispered.

Eleanor nodded.

"Did you go this past one, too?"

To my surprise, Eleanor's eyes clouded with tears. The woman rarely displayed emotions, and in less than one week, I'd seen her tear up twice. "I did. And I can tell you Kendrick Paulson is way too ill to do what he's been charged with. The man could barely walk across the living room to let me inside. Crazy or not, he ain't the one who killed Martha Cayhill."

I turned into the parking lot of La Hacienda and pulled next to my car. Eleanor reached for the door handle but I stopped her. Between what Cliff told me and now Eleanor's words, my head spun. "What else do you know that you aren't telling me?"

Eleanor looked over at me, her face a sea of emotions. The biggest one was fear. "That my original worries about you being in danger are right on target."

"What do you mean?"

"I mean, Renee, is if an old man who's on his last legs as cancer eats his insides up can get arrested in this town for murder, then anything is possible. People are going to great lengths to hide things, and they're willing to offer u p s acrifices to ge t wh at th ey wa nt. I don't want you to be the next one."

My stomach dropped. "Cancer? What kind of cancer?"

"Prostate. Stage 4. Kendrick's got maybe two weeks to live, and the poor man will spend them inside a jail cell."

Eleanor exited the SUV and walked to my car. I let her go without saying another word, because frankly, I was too freaked out to speak.

I followed Eleanor back to her house, wondering what really was going on. When she mentioned Stage 4 prostate cancer, something sinister wormed around inside my head. Was it even possible? Plausible? Accomplishable?

Was County J udge Harold Singleton involved in all this? And was he faking being ill? If so, why? What lengths were people willing to go to just to have a new business in the county?

By the time I pulled up behind Eleanor at her house, I was shaking so hard I could barely hold onto the steering wheel.

It seemed Cliff and Eleanor were on target and that I was in danger though I still was in the dark as to why.

And, I'd just left my protection in a confused cloud of dust at Ten Mile Cemetery.

Shit.

ONCE BACK INSIDE the house, I went straight to the bathroom. Eleanor didn't question me, only gave me a worried look as I limped past her. I soaked in the hot water until it turned cold.

While dressing, I heard the noise of the television, so I slipped out into the hall, hoping I'd find Eleanor asleep on the couch. Sure enough, curled under a warm throw, Eleanor was lightly snoring, out like a little kid worn out from a stressful day.

I went back into my room and stretched out on the bed, almost wishing I still had some pain pills. Grabbing my phone, surprised to see it was after eleven, I mulled over what to say in a text to Cliff. While pondering what nuggets of gold I should type to lure him back after being so rude earlier, a noise outside caught my attention. Groaning as I rolled over and reached for the curtains, a hint of excitement at thinking it was Cliff doing a drive-by, my heart thudded.

It was a vehicle alright, but not Cliff's.

The big, black SUV slowed to a crawl less than thirty feet from Eleanor's driveway. The streetlight gleamed off the shiny paint and tinted windows. The passenger window rolled down and a hand tossed something on the ground. The SUV backed up the road and disappeared down the road.

This was certainly not a good time for Eleanor's house to be the lone one off a windy, back road no one ever came down. No one except the cop I'd told to get lost and now, someone in a vehicle that probably cost more than my house was worth who'd left a little gift in the drive.

I cursed Arkansas' stupid law requiring vehicles to only have license plates on the back. The only description I could give was it was a black SUV.

I didn't have to get up and go look to see if I was right. I *knew* something sinister sat outside, and had zero interest in going out alone to check it out. Instead, I sent a text to Cliff.

"Just had a visit from Men in Black. Um, can we just pretend I never said I didn't need protection? Because I just became a believer. They even left me a package."

Alone under the covers, heart pounding and mind racing, I nearly jumped off the bed when my phone buzzed.

"Lock the doors and stay inside. I'll be right over."

Thank God.

What kind of new Hell awaited outside?

"Yeah, go to Suicide Lake and end it all, Renee. Brilliant fucking idea. Only I could screw up killing myself and wind up in the middle of some weird conspiracy."

CLIFF MADE IT to Eleanor's in less than five minutes from across town. Though he didn't turn the siren on, the blue lights lit up the dark evening sky as he came tearing down Eleanor's road. The second I saw him pull in, I met him outside. At least this time I was in a new robe and slippers.

The package the goons in the black SUV left behind was not a package at all. Cliff put on gloves and picked the small, unsealed envelope off the driveway and a piece of paper fluttered to the ground.

Walking closer, no longer afraid of a simple slip of paper, I asked, "What does it say?"

Cliff squinted while holding the paper

near the headlights of his car. "It's a picture with nothing written on it. Do you know who either one of them are? Sort of looks like it was taken at Bradford Lake."

Pausing next to him, I leaned down to get a better look.

I wish I hadn't because the image made my head spin. How was it possible? Where did those freaks get the picture, and why did they bring it here and just leave it behind?

"Renee, oh, shit. Sit down," Cliff said, grabbing my arm. He led me to the passenger side of his unit and gently eased me down in the seat. "You know who they are, don't you?"

Tears ran down my cheeks and I couldn't stop shaking even though I had a warm robe on and Cliff's extra jacket over my shoulders. What was I going to do now? I wanted to kick myself for being such a wuss before and not going outside and getting the note myself. But no, I chickened out and called in the one and only person—besides Eleanor—I dreaded finding out the truth about my family's past.

179

"Renee, breathe. Look at me," Cliff cooed. I refused to comply, continuing to stare down at my feet. He crouched in front of me and tried again. "Look at me. I'm here, just like I said I'd be. You can't pressure me to leave again, not like before. Tell me what's going on and who these people are, and why seeing them has frightened you so much."

"Guess you'll find out soon enough. You'll eat those words the minute I tell you," I whispered.

Cliff's hands rested on my knees. They were warm, strong, and comforting. He rubbed them across my legs and said, "I promise you, Renee Michelle Thornton, I'm not going anywhere except where you go. Talk to me."

I lost it and the tears turned into sobs. "My dad...and his girlfriend," I finally choked out.

"Oh, shit."

Cliff sounded as shocked as I felt. He reached past me and grabbed a box of tissue from the floorboard. After wiping my nose and eyes, I continued. "Yeah. Cyndi

Robertson was her name. I believe you're right about the location, though I have no idea where the picture came from. I promise you my mother certainly didn't take it. I've never seen it before, but that's definitely my dad and Cyndi."

"Any idea when it was taken?"

"Judging by his hair and what he's wearing, about a month before they disappeared. Mom made him that scarf. Gave it to him for his birthday, which was two months before..."

I couldn't say it. The word was on the tip of my tongue but wouldn't leave. Once I said it, everything I knew, all the hopes and dreams I had during the last few days, foolishly thinking I might have a real shot at love, would vanish.

Thankfully, the intelligent, kindhearted, and warm soul in front of me figured it out. I knew he did—could see the wheels spinning and then the *Ah-ha!* moment lit up his eyes. The excitement of solving a puzzle was replaced by a sadness.

Don't say it, Cliff. Please? Don't speak it

into existence between the two of us. Let's just sit here and pretend you stopped by for a warm kiss on a cold night. A hot cup of coffee to heat the insides, and maybe some skin-on-skin to sizzle the outside.

"They're dead, aren't they?

Damn. My fairy tale, make-believe bubble just popped. "Yes. I'm pretty sure their remains are at the bottom of Suicide Lake, at least that's what my mother told me."

Cliff rocked back on his heels. "Jesus, Mary, and Joseph."

"Am I going to get in trouble for not telling a cop sooner? You know, that I'm pretty sure my mom killed two people?"

"This isn't police business. This is *our* business. Our *private* business. If only the two of us were aware, my answer would be to never think or worry about it again. He...disappeared over thirty years, right? Before I moved to town?"

"Yeah. A magical wand masquerading as a tire iron was waved and poof! They vanished," I muttered.

"Then we need to concentrate on who

else knew and why they are trying to scare you. Any ideas?"

I could only think of one, and dropping the earth-shattering news in Cliff's lap was risky. Jobs weren't the only thing at stake now. Lives were. Our lives. Eleanor's life. I knew it. Felt it in the deepest recesses of my heart.

"Yeah, I've got a pretty good lead, but it's going to take a bit to tell you all of it. Want to wait until you finish your shift?"

Cliff helped me out of the seat and pulled me into a warm hug. I melted into his embrace, wishing I could climb inside his jacket and hide away the rest of the night, nestled against his skin.

"I only took this job because I was bored after retiring from the military, so if I lose it, no big deal. I'll just radio in that I'm taking a late dinner break. No rule in the handbook that states *where* I have to eat. So, I'm all yours."

"Can we sit back inside? I'm freezing, and don't want to go in the house. Eleanor would freak if she heard what I'm about to tell you."

183

"Of course," Cliff said, then chuckled softly as he walked to the other side.

I glared at him when he sat behind the driver's seat. "Something about this strikes you as funny?"

"No, well, sort of. I've been waiting for months to get you alone in my car at night—you know—so I could ravish you under the moon? Now, here you are and about to dump news on my I have the sneaky suspicion might just rock this town to its core. Guess I should have been more specific about *why* you were in my car when I wished for it to happen."

"I've learned the same lesson lately. Wishes need to be spelled out. Every word. God, Cliff, are you sure you want to know? Last chance to back out."

Clifton Robert Simpson—the first boy I'd ever kissed and truly loved—took my hand and wound his fingers through my own, smiled that sexy lopsided grin, and said, "There's nowhere else I'm supposed to be than right here with you, Renee. Always."

Smiling through my tears, I cleared my throat and told him all I knew.

Every single detail I remembered.

Chapter Eleven

"I'LL MAKE THE call and get things all set up. In the meantime, you need to keep your cell with you everywhere. Bathroom, bedroom, car, kitchen. Everywhere. Stay here at Eleanor's and don't go to work tomorrow. It's too dangerous. When I get off duty, I'll come back and we'll get you moved into my house."

"Cliff, I can't do that, I've still got Traci's SUV. I promised I'd pick her up in the morning. Besides, if I suddenly don't show up for work, they'll know something's wrong. Plus, if the mayor is out of the office again tomorrow, I might be able to snoop around some. You know, find out some more information on the land deal? And I don't want to leave Eleanor's just yet. What if she's in danger, too?"

Cliff shook his head. " No way. Too dangerous. I can't keep an eye on you while you're at work. They'd really think something was wrong if I showed up and sat in the lobby all day, which is the only way I'd let you go."

"I appreciate your concern and all your suggestions, Cliff, but you're sneaking back into the stalker category again. I'll be fine, especially after you set up the interview. How long do you think it'll take your friend to get us—"

Cliff's phone vibrated and he smiled. "Not long at all. Jared's an old army buddy. Knew I could count on him. Oh, great. He's got us scheduled to meet him and Charles Glenn tomorrow night at seven. They'll come to my place, and so will you until all this gets sorted out."

Sensing I was losing the battle of wills, I conceded. "I'll agree to stay with you as long as you agree to let me go to work. At least tomorrow."

He grinned. "Always a negotiator. Okay, if you insist on going to work then you leave me with no choice but to make you wear a wire."

I gaped at him. "Are you serious? No, no way. I'll be nervous enough as it is. I'm not cut out for playing a spy full-throttle."

"Don't worry, Renee. Technology has advanced to the point recording devices are really small. I have some at home, one that actually looks like a nice piece of jewelry. I'll go get it and leave it in the mailbox."

Groaning, I muttered, "Fine, but I doubt the Mayor is stupid enough to say anything at work to me incriminating. Hell, he might not even be there tomorrow."

"Oh, he'll be there. You mark my words. So will reporters. His wife's killer was arrested, remember? I guarantee you he'll be right in front of the cameras, assuring folks Whitten County is safe once again."

"You think?"

"Yep. If all this mess is because of a secret land deal, and it almost fell through because of the discovery of Martha's body at the lake, he needs to put up some good PR."

I sighed and stared out the window. Though relieved after dumping the sordid story out to Cliff, I s till f elt off. Things—memories—were jumbled around inside my head. I was too old for this shit.

Cliff n oticed m y u nease. H e k issed my cheek and whispered, "I promise to behave when you're at my house. At least until all this is over. Then, all bets are off."

I chuckled, "Sex isn't the answer for every woe, Cliff. Actually, it's last on my list of priorities for a variety of reasons. I just...I don't understand why you're still here after what I told you. You're entangled in this web of deceit and lies now, and I hate that."

"I don't," Cliff murmured while nuzzling my neck. "Excitement, intrigue, and a hot woman to pursue. What more can a man ask for?"

Pulling away, I laughed. "You're too much, Cliff. Too much."

Winking, Cliff responded, "I hope you say those very same words when you see me naked."

"Ditto," I said, smiling as I exited the car. "One more question then I've got to get some sleep. Oh, who am I kidding? I'm so keyed up I'll probably just stare at the ceiling all night. So, back to my question. Are you sure I should come stay with you? Don't you think we're being watched?"

"Of course we are, which means the Mayor and his partners in crime are already aware. When they realize you've got protection, they'll back off. At least long enough for us to meet with Jared and Charles."

I felt sick to my stomach. "You're sure they won't arrest me after I tell them...you know...about Dad and Cyndi?"

Cliff grimaced. "We already went over how to handle that, remember? Just stick to what I told you and you'll be fine. Promise. You don't think I'd steer you wrong, do you?"

"If you are, then when I die, I'm coming back to haunt you. Forever."

Cliff's l aughter l ingered l ong a fter he drove away. I walked back inside and locked the door and went to check on Eleanor. She was still out cold on the couch, so I slipped back to my room and took another hot shower.

Minutes later, covered pulled up to my chin, I stared at the ceiling, wondering just how I'd pull all this off without falling apart.

"Guess you'll find out what you're made of tomorrow, Renee."

AFTER LEAVING ELEANOR'S, I pulled over at the gas station and read the instructions Cliff left for me about the lapel pin. It took me a few minutes, but I managed to turn it on and secure it to my shirt. The temperature hovered near the freezing mark outside and I was sweating like it was ninety-five.

"If you're listening, I'm sure you can hear the sweat pour out of me," I muttered.

Pulling back on the main road, I headed to Traci's. Bypassing downtown, I took the back roads, fearing reporters had already descended. Like a crazy woman, I randomly chatted as though Cliff was sitting next to me. I wasn't much of a talker unless I was nervous.

And wow, was I nervous. By the time I made it to Traci's, my heart was pounding.

Traci was waiting on the front porch. After parking, I got out but she motioned for me to stop. "Please, you drive. My head's killing me."

"Oh, sure thing. Hangovers suck," I replied while climbing back behind the wheel. "Did you drink some water? That'll help."

Traci slid into the seat and groaned. "Water, coffee, and about four aspirins. So far, nothing's worked. Work will be a blast."

I tried to miss the holes in the road for a smoother ride. My head didn't feel so great, either, though my issue wasn't from booze. I was exhausted. My prediction of staring at the ceiling all night came true. I didn't get one lick of sleep.

Once on Highway 9, my hands started shaking again. In less than fifteen minutes, we'd be at work and my new role as a spy would begin. "Guess I owe you an apology."

"What for?"

"Letting you drink too much."

Traci waved her hand. "Please. I'm a big girl and it's my own fault. Besides, I never listened to Edward when he would bitch at me to slow down, so I doubt I'da listened to you. Oh, and I'm the one who owes you an apology."

"For what?"

"Having to drive home a drunk and for listening to me blabber on about my life. Dumping out shit I should've kept to myself. So, sorry."

"Not necessary. I mean, what are friends for, right?"

Traci smiled and patted my hand. "I'm serious. You let me go on and on about my crazy world and I barely gave you a chance to talk about yours. So, since I'm no longer trashed, I'm listening."

Knowing Cliff was listening, or if he wasn't tuned in live he could play it back later—a sick feeling churned in my stomach. I had to be careful what I said because there was a lot about my past I hadn't told him. I mean, he said he kept up with me while he was gone, but that didn't guarantee he knew intimate details.

"Not much more to tell other than what I did already," I answered.

"Renee, that's horseshit. You've been through Hell! Your dad left, your mom died, you got pregnant in high school, lost the baby, and married a monster who beat the crap out of you for years. That's just skimming the surface. How long have you hidden your real pain below dark waters? I remember how devastated you were when your dad left."

The comment sent shivers up my spine.

"Long enough to know I don't really like rehashing it."

"Is that why you didn't testify during Billy's trial?"

I almost ran off the road. Traci's choice of words struck a nerve. "Excuse me?"

"Not wanting to dredge up painful memories. Is that why you didn't attend his murder trial? I mean, he did kill his wife."

Seething anger licked a fire in my gut. I took a few deep breaths before I said something I'd regret later. "I'm well aware of what Billy Runsford did. Not only to his wife, but me. To say I'm terrified of the man is the understatement of the century. It's taken me *years* to actually speak his name without having a panic attack. So pardon me for being a coward."

"Oh, honey, I didn't mean it like that! Gosh, I've upset you and I was only trying to give you a friendly ear to vent to. Good thing I didn't pick counselor as my career choice. I obviously suck at it."

"Since you brought the subject up, I've got a question for you. You mentioned you kept up with all the fun and exciting news in Ridgeport while you were away, so if you were so concerned about being a friend, why didn't you pick up the phone and call me?"

The color from Traci's cheeks vanished. "I...uh...well, I wanted to but—"

"But you didn't. You just buried your head in the sand like everyone else around this fucking town. I get that. You had your own life to live, a family to raise, who wants to hear someone else's woes, right? Poor little white trash got what she deserved, right? Another small town whore who got knocked up before seventeen. Daddy abandoned her and was left to care for the drunken, former homecoming queen. What did Gretchen say last night? Ah, yes, that being friends with me would just drag a person down. Just like everyone else in my life, you abandoned me. Don't worry though, I'm over it. Happened a long time ago."

"Renee, please, I didn't mean to hurt you—"

"Hey, you opened this can, remember?" I interrupted, the anger inside me controlling my words. "Yes, I've lived through some very trying times. Lost all those I loved and was trapped in a violent marriage until Billy grew tired of hitting me and found a new toy to smack around. Unfortunately, he broke his new toy permanently. But you know what? I dealt with all the crap after being forced to by doctors and counselors, remember? Oh, wait, I seem to recall that after my first trip to the looney bin, you steered clear. Already had my brain probed and prodded by professionals who insisted I talk about my experiences, so I'm good."

Heavy silence fell between the two of us for a few minutes. Tears filled m y e yes s o I pulled over on the shoulder before I wrecked and killed us both. "You'll need to drive the rest of the way," I mumbled.

Switching seats without a word spoken, Traci finally c leared h er t hroat a nd reached out for me. "Renee, I'm so sorry. I was just a kid, too, and didn't know how to handle all that was going on in your life. Yes, I steered clear, but not because I didn't care about you. I just didn't know what to say. I mean, you were so strong before. You got a job, helped your mom out, never cried or complained about your dad leaving, so when you flipped after losing the baby, I was at a loss as to how to deal. Saying sorry now seems pathetic and trite, I know, but I truly am. And I'm here, now."

Swallowing hard, I pushed her hand away and motioned for her to drive. "We're going to be late and I have nothing left to say, except I won't need a ride home after work."

Traci looked at me with a mixture of pity and sadness. It was the same look I'd seen my entire life from others and I hated it. Turning my face to stare out the window, I dabbed my eyes on my jacket.

We didn't speak again the rest of the drive to work. The interaction reminded why I didn't have any close friends. People lied all the time. Professed their undying love and devotion until turning blue in the face, yet did a flip-flop when hard times came. I was better off on my own.

Traci pulled into the parking lot, the place was crammed with people.

And news vans.

And Mayor Cayhill's car.

Joy.

I didn't wait for Traci. Stepping out of her vehicle, I headed in the back door then straight to the restroom to fix my smeared makeup.

THE REST OF the day was strange. The atmosphere of the office was full of excitement and sadness. Cliff was on target with his predictions. Mayor Cayhill gave a nice little speech from his desk to a packed room full of eager reporters as Detective Greenwood looked on. He made sure to thank all those involved in the investigation of his beloved wife, spoke of how justice would prevail, and what a wonderful, compassionate group of people lived in Ridgeport and Whitten County.

Traci and I never spoke during the full

eight hours. After Mayor Cayhill did his best to smooth safety concerns to all of Whitten County's residents—and I'm sure to the secret investors who were surely watching the live broadcast—Traci spent most of the afternoon inside his office. The other two employees huddled by themselves in the copy room, grousing and gossiping about the arrests of crazy Kendrick Paulson, Jr.

My day was spent answering the phones which rang incessantly. I'd taken over one-hundred calls from residents, most wanting to offer condolences to the Mayor. Unwilling to interrupt the little pow-wow between Traci and the Mayor, I took messages. By the time four o'clock rolled around, the stack of pink paper was several inches high.

During the news conference, I took the opportunity to send Cliff a text, mentioning I'd need a ride home after work. His response almost made me laugh out loud but I contained myself.

"Figured. I doubt Traci Rogers will ever want you in her vehicle again."

It was four-twenty and the phones were

finally quiet. Shari and Myrtle decided they'd gabbed each other's ears off enough and left the copy room. They both ignored me as they walked to their desks and shut their computers down. Hateful old skanks. They'd both worked for the Mayor for years and weren't friendly or helpful at all to new employees, including Traci. She'd mentioned my first day they were both quite territorial and she was right.

Both women left without saying goodbye and I didn't care. They were gone, Traci was still in with the mayor, and I had ten minutes to kill before Cliff came to pick me up. Instead of sitting still, I decided to use the opportunity of an empty office. While walking to the filing room, sirens wailed outside. One right after another, which usually meant an ugly wreck on the interstate.

I poked around in the files but didn't find anything that screamed "Hey, pick me up! Incriminating document here!" Then again, I had no clue what I should be looking for, so I gave up and went back to my desk.

The second I sat down, Traci opened the door and exited Mayor Cayhill's office. She looked like she'd just spent the afternoon in the principal's office. She walked past me like I wasn't there, grabbed her purse, and left. By the sound of her footsteps, it sounded like she was running.

My phone vibrated in my hand and I jumped. Jesus, I was a bundle of raw nerves, and knowing I was stuck inside the office with only Mayor Cayhill made my throat dry. I stood, snatched up my purse, and headed to the front door while trying to read the text from Cliff.

"Big wreck on I-30 overpass. Stuck in traffic. Be there soon. You okay?"

Damn!

Panic roared up inside me, wondering how long I'd have to wait outside.

"Renee? A moment please?"

Turning, I felt my knees go weak when I saw Mayor Cayhill stood less than three feet away. The look on his face was downright terrifying. Gone was the warm countenance from before, replaced by a stern look of anger.

No way was I going to be alone with him. I reached the front door and tried to open it, but it was locked.

"It's locked, Renee. I asked Traci to make sure we had no interruptions while we have ourselves a long chat."

Oh, God!

Cliff never mentioned exactly how the recording device worked, so I said a silent prayer it somehow went to his phone and he was listening.

"I know you're waiting for Deputy Simpson to come fetch you, but I'm afraid he's going to be late. Stuck in traffic, you know."

The eeriness in the Mayor's voice made my head spin. I straightened my shoulders and faced him, hoping he'd say something incriminating since it was all being recorded—and he had no clue. "One I'm sure wasn't an actual accident, correct?"

Mayor Cayhill grinned wide. "Correct.

You catch on quick, Renee. Unfortunately, not quick enough."

Detective Greenwood emerged from the other side of the door. Before I could even utter a sound, he was one me. Yanking my cell away, he tossed it to the floor and stomped on it. The sounds of the shattering plastic and glass sent waves of fear pulsing through my chest.

"That was rude, Detective. If you wanted to borrow my phone, you could've simply asked."

"Silence that mouth of hers until I'm ready to hear her speak again," Mayor Cayhill snarled.

I tried to run, pushing past the pain in my back, forcing my limbs to listen to me. I made it less than five feet down the hallway, my shoes making a weird sound on the marble floor, before Detective Greenwood grabbed a handful of my hair.

He spun me around. I clawed at his face but he was so much bigger than I was, it didn't matter. When his big hand balled up into a fist, the years of abuse from Billy took over.

Instead of fighting b ack, I cowered, watching his fist come toward my face in slow motion, praying the first h it w ould be enough to kill me.

"Gladly, sir," Detective Greenwood muttered.

Red, hot pain burst inside my head as stars replaced the images of the detective, City Hall, and the Mayor.

"TIME TO WAKE up, Renee. We're all set up for our chat now."

The ammonia stench under my nose jerked me out of unconsciousness. It took a few seconds for me to get my bearings. Once the burn of ammonia disappeared, it was replaced by a familiar scent it took me a full minute to recognize.

Traci's perfume.

The heavy, dull throb in my right jaw

reminded me of the last beating I took from Billy, and being knocked out somehow dislodged dark, twisted memories from my past. Things I'd shelved and blamed on others, unwilling to let the truth rumble inside my mind.

Thirty-three years of mental anguish, blocked from my thoughts, only appearing in my nightmares, were free.

I knew why I was here, how all this tied to me, and exactly how I'd use my own dark secret to my advantage. The punch dislodged hidden memories, ones I'd jumbled up inside my mind. The conversation with my mother the night I was sixteen roared back and this time, I remembered it the correct way, rather than how I wanted the truth to be.

I'd been the one who came clean about Dad and Cyndi after coming home from work and listening to Mom sob about being alone. My confession broke Mom's spirit and drove her to hit the bottle even harder. My mother's death was on my hands, just like the others.

"Get her into a chair," Mayor Cayhill barked.

Rough hands untied the rope around my wrists. I knew without looking they belonged to Greenwood. Plastic rustled as he picked me up from Traci's bed and shoved me onto a chair in the middle of her living room.

Rubbing my sore wrists, I glanced past Greenwood and Cayhill and over at Traci. She stood in the doorway leading to the kitchen, a cigarette in her shaking hands. Her big eyes were wild with fright and determination. Maybe a hint of remorse. Her beauty was overshadowed by her dark intentions. I gave her a wicked grin and said, "I've got a new nickname for you. Traci the Twat. Fits you perfectly. Wonder if your aunt Sylvia would approve of you killing me on her property?"

"Hurry up and get this over with," Traci muttered then turned and disappeared into the dark kitchen.

"Ladies, let's not be hateful. We are here together to discuss business. No sense in making our time difficult."

I laughed at the mayor's words and saw a glint of anger sparkle behind his eyes, "Yep. Politician from head to toe, even when on the cusp of killing someone. Did you use the same tactic on your wife, or just jump her from behind?"

Greenwood tensed up but Cayhill threw his head back and laughed. "You've known all along, haven't you?"

"Actually, no. Not even when Traci tried to pull information from me last night and this morning. Was that your idea, Mayor?"

"It was."

"Too bad you opted to rely on words rather than pain to get the information you wanted. Not good planning on your part. Abuse victims respond to fear, not kindness. When Greenwood stuck his fist in my face, I remembered things I buried years ago."

Mayor Cayhill narrowed his eyes while studying my face. A look of surprise beamed on his forehead. "Are you trying to say all this time, you didn't know?"

I smiled. "I'm not trying to say it. I just did."

"She's lying, Peyton," Greenwood interjected.

Cayhill shook his head. "No, Richard, I don't think she is. Perhaps we miscalculated a few points."

"Oh, you did. Your first mistake was killing your wife. The second was involving me. The third was framing an innocent man. All because your wife was a whore, Peyton."

Cayhill stiffened. Greenwood stood but remained in place when the Mayor held up his hand. "Harsh words coming from the likes of you, Ms. Thornton. If your drunk mother could have kept her man satisfied in the bedroom, we wouldn't be here right now."

"Tell me something I don't already know! Something like why did you wait so long to kill your wife if you knew about what happened? This all ties back to the land deal, so why risk putting her in the lake? Why didn't you just make her disappear?"

"You are smarter than I gave you credit for, but you aren't schooled in the ways of making even nasty situations come out smelling clean. Had I known years ago what my wife had been up to, I would have done something...permanent about it. Alas, I was too caught up in running our lovely city, doing my best to bring in new revenue, to notice she was out spreading her legs all over town."

"Then I guess you aren't as smart as what you've painted inside your own head," I said.

"Touché, Ms. Thornton. It hurt me deeply when my beloved Martha broke down and told me the sordid tale. I had just shared with her over dinner the exciting news about the manufacturing plant, and how wonderful it would be to get rid of the county's eyesore known as Bradford Lake. I'm sure you understand why she became so upset. Unfortunately, I didn't take the news of her past transgressions very well. I was forced to call in a favor owed to me by Detective Greenwood to help...make things go away. Too bad you decided to end your life that night and discovered her body. That was supposed to happen when the lake was drained. By then, my whoring bride would have been nothing but bones, and her death ruled yet another tragedy at Suicide Lake."

"Peyton!" Greenwood grumbled. "Enough chatting. Let's just get this over and done."

I turned my attention over to Greenwood as the missing piece of the puzzle fell into place. "Your wife didn't move to California, did she? You killed her and dumped her in the lake, too, and Cayhill knew about it!"

"I said enough!" Greenwood yelled. In seconds, he was across the room and yanked me out of the chair by my arm. "Traci! Give me the pills and some water."

"Oh, God, I can't handle this!" Traci moaned from the kitchen.

Dancing close to madness, I laughed so hard tears rolled down my cheeks. "You saved Eleanor's pills? Brilliant! Good luck forcing me to swallow them."

"Oh, you will, bitch. You will," Greenwood muttered. "And trust me, I'll enjoy shoving them down your throat. Help you finish what you started. It's all your fault things got screwed up anyway!"

"Wait!" Cayhill yelled. "We need to know what's she's told Simpson first."

"What is...oh, fuck! She's wired!" Greenwood stuttered. He ripped the pin off my shirt at the same time the back of his hand connected with my head. "Fuck!"

Stunned by the impact of my head slamming into the hardwood, I heard the crunch of Greenwood's boots crush the recording device. Traci flew f rom the kitchen, a million questions tumbling from her mouth. Cayhill shoved Greenwood aside, bent down, and grabbed a handful of my hair. Pulling me up from the floor, he shoved his face inches from mine. "Your death will be painful, now, and no one will ever find your body!"

The sound of the front door crashing in barely registered. All my attention was focused on the crazed eyes of the man breathing hard into my face. Though much older and eyes a different c olor, I s aw the same look in Billy's eyes when he was in a rage-fueled state. Anger and hatred erupted from me. I spit into those ugly eyes while landing a solid kick to the old bastard's groin. The kick was hard enough to make him let go and I fell to the floor.

"Fuck you," I whispered.

"Hands up, all of you!"

In a rush of footsteps and screaming, it was over. A horde of men in state trooper uniforms burst in, cuffing the deadly trio in seconds. Warm arms scooped me up from the floor, the sweet, worried voice of Cliff cooed to me while carrying me outside.

"Baby, you okay?"

Nodding after he set me down in the front seat of his truck, I glanced around. Traci's yard was crammed full of numerous undercover cop cars, not one of them with lights on. The look of terror on Cliff's face for my safety was almost funny. He looked like he'd seen a ghost. "Took you long enough," I muttered.

Too shaken to respond, Cliff shut the door and ran around the truck. I heard him mumble something to another officer before opening the door. Once inside the cab, he gunned the engine and took off.

"I'm taking you to the hospital. Told the detective he'd just have to wait until tomorrow to question you. Then, you're coming home with me. No arguments."

Leaning my head against the neck rest, I sighed and didn't offer one up.

"I'M FINE, ELEANOR. Really. A little sore and a lot tired but fine. Just a slight concussion and some bruises. Please, go get some rest."

Eleanor sat at the edge of Cliff's bed, clutching my hand like I was a balloon about to float away. I wanted to kick Cliff for calling her but he insisted. Again, I didn't argue because I knew he was right. She'd hear the news from someone else and flip out. Better to hear it from Cliff with assurances I was fine.

"Cliff made up the bed in the guestroom,

216

so if you need me, I'll be right across the hall."

"Thank you. I won't. Promise. In ten minutes, I'll be out."

Eleanor stood as Cliff walked in. She walked over and hugged him tight, muttering something in his ear. Though I couldn't hear what she said, it must have been something sentimental because Cliff blushed.

Once she was gone, Cliff eased himself down next to me. Opening his arms wide, I snuggled up against his chest.

"You're safe now, Renee. It's all over. Sleep, my love."

Cliff fell asleep before I did. In the dark, I closed my eyes and listened to the beat of his heart and each steady, rhythmic breath. The events of the evening tried to overtake my mind, but I pushed the hatefulness away. Instead, I focused on what a blessing Cliff's presence in my life turned out to be.

What we had now went way beyond kindness shown to an old friend, or stolen kisses between two adults attempting to rekindle a teenage romance. Cliff followed his instincts and saved me, even though I pushed him away several times. He could have just given up and never come back to me.

But he didn't.

And that meant more to me than I would ever be able to express to him because it had never happened to me before. The man never blinked, never wavered, even when I told him the dark, ugly secrets of my past.

Soaking in the warmth of his body, I felt my mind drift, wondering what it would be like to sleep next to him after making love. Was this what my life could be like now? Forever? Would this bond last if he knew...everything?

I KNEW I was dreaming the moment I stepped forward and didn't feel the damp grass from an earlier rain shower under my bare feet. Instead of fighting to wake myself up as I'd done for over thirty-six years, I let the dream unfold—just like it happened.

The moon was full and bright, the rays casting silver shimmers like pretty stardust across the top of the water. It was late summer and the night air heavy with humidity. The sweet perfume of magnolias and honeysuckle tickled my nose as I watched, crouched in the shadows.

The three bodies were tangled together, writhing naked on top of one of Mom's sheets the cheating bastard stole from the closet. The things they were doing to each other made me sick to my stomach. I'd caught my parents once making love when I woke up from thunder booming outside and ran to their bedroom.

What the three in front of me were doing wasn't sweet, or romantic, or even understandable. It was disturbing and vile.

And it angered me.

Mom loved him with all she had. Every single fiber in Caroline Clark's being vibrated and lived for Raymond Thornton. The way she took care of him, kept the house, fixed d ecent m eals o n a shoestring budget. The way her eyes lit up when he walked in from work like he was Prince Charming arriving on his white horse, ready to sweep her off her feet.

Mom's eyes had taken on a new look. A wounded, heartbroken one when she broke down and cried earlier at the kitchen table after a terrible fight with Daddy. I didn't hear what they said, only the angry tones in both their voices. When things quieted down, I peeked out my bedroom door and saw Daddy take one of Mom's sheets and leave.

"I'm going to the lake, Caroline. Gotta clear my head," he'd yelled before starting up his bike.

I'd gone to the kitchen to check on Mom. Here lovely eyes clouded over with tears as she told me she feared we'd have to move soon because Daddy wouldn't be around much longer.

"Daddy loves someone else, Renee. Not me! He'll make us leave soon, and I don't know where we'll go. I can't afford rent somewhere else."

Mom didn't say anything else. She couldn't, because she'd passed out from too much alcohol, leaving me alone and terrified in the house.

Not for long.

I went to the garage, grabbed my bicycle, and the tire iron on Daddy's workbench. I kept to the dark shadows and away from the streetlights while peddling as fast as my legs would go. By the time I made it to Bradford Lake, it was dark.

Clutching the tire iron like a club, ignoring the mosquitoes biting me, I watched Daddy touch and poke the two sluts while they groaned and giggled. The blonde one sitting on Daddy's face I recognized as Cyndi Roberston. The other one with the dark, mahogany hair, had her face buried in Daddy's crotch.

Cyndi stood, took a drink from a wine bottle, and stumbled away from the others. "You're wearing me out, Raymond! I'm sweating like crazy! Let me go rinse off real quick and I'll be right back. You take care of him while I'm gone, sweetie. Save some of that tongue action for me!"

Cyndi bobbed and weaved her way over the grass until she made it to the dock. When she passed my hiding spot, I didn't breathe. I waited until I heard her run down to the end of the boardwalk and the rustle of the water before I stood and followed.

Clouds rolled over the moon just as Cyndi put her hands on the dock to pull herself out of the water. I wasn't going to let this woman ruin my mom's life, so I took my stance, tire iron above my head like a baseball bat.

Once Cyndi was out of the water yet still on her belly, I smashed her head in. The dull thud and small *oomph* she let out barely registered in my ears. She quit making any noise after the fifth time I hit her, so I left her and ran back to my hiding spot.

I didn't have to wait long for Daddy to come looking for her. He screamed when he got to the edge of the dock and saw what I did to his whore. He was so concerned about her—rather than me and Mom like he should be—he fell down and cried while trying to pick her up.

He didn't hear me coming, either.

It took eight swings to make him stop yelling.

Both of them were heavy so it took me a bit to push them off the edge of the dock into the water.

"Oh, my God! What have you done!"

The other woman stood at the edge of the lake. She was dressed now in a thin, sleeveless cotton dress, her exposed skin as white as though she were a ghost. She didn't run to help the two she'd spent so much intimate time with earlier. Instead, she stared at me for a split second before turning and running through the woods.

I made the decision not to chase her down. She was on foot, a long way from town, and she didn't see my face long enough to give a good description. Just to be safe, in case she did run for help, I ran to Daddy's bike, took the sheet and the remaining clothes, and wrapped them up tight around the handlebars. Then I pushed the bike down the boardwalk until it fell off t he e dge and joined Daddy and Cyndi.

Mom always said Bradford Lake was deep and dangerous and the boardwalk would lead to oblivion if someone fell off it.

She was right.

I WOKE UP with a start and covered in sweat. For a second, I didn't know where I was until Cliff stirred next to me.

"Shh, baby, I'm here."

He followed the murmur by pulling me tighter to his chest. Tears ran down my face, soaking his chest in seconds. The need to wake him and come clean about my father competed with the urge to keep quiet and not ruin the one and only good thing I'd ever experienced in my life. Inside my mind, I cursed Detective Dick. Had he not knocked loose memories I didn't want to recall, I wouldn't be a bundle of nerves while trying to come to grips with the truth about the night I was thirteen.

Yes, I'd committed murder. Twice. Would have killed the third person that night as well had she not run away. Knowing her identity now made me shudder. Martha kept the secret all these years as well, then panicked when Peyton told her the lake was to be drained. God, so much deceit and lies!

No, I wouldn't tell Cliff. Some secrets were best kept hidden beneath Suicide Lake.

Chapter Thirteen

"TOLD YOU IT wouldn't take long. They got all they really needed from the recordings. Good thing the battery didn't conk out."

Cliff held the door open and we stepped outside. The afternoon air was pleasant, a light breeze chasing the clouds away. We'd been at the state police headquarters for almost three hours, each telling the investigators our parts of the story.

"True, and that Greenwood didn't find it sooner! So, how long will it be before they release Kendrick from jail?"

"Probably by the end of the day. Charles told me they just picked up Judge Singleton while we were inside. I guarantee you Ridgeport's gossip lines are burned up!"

"No doubt. I'm tired but I dread going back home. I'm sure reporters are around every corner, just waiting to pounce on us. So many people were involved in this mess, even Judge Singleton."

"They stopped at nothing to get their hands on a lot of money, that's for sure." Cliff opened the door to his truck and helped me inside. "That's why I plan on taking you to dinner up here first. We need some peace and quiet after all this. Besides, I, um, have some things I need to tell you."

He shut the door before I could say anything. The tone of his voice made me shiver. When he climbed in the truck, he changed the subject and asked where I'd like to eat. I didn't press the issue, figuring I'd find out what he had on his mind soon enough.

We settled on Italian food and Cliff drove around until he found a quaint restaurant off Highway 5 near Saline County. Since it was only four o'clock, the place was practically empty. The waiter escorted us to a secluded booth, we ordered and munched on bread dipped in marinara sauce, then Cliff cleared his throat. I looked up and saw the worry behind his eyes and felt a pang of sadness stab into my heart.

"Listen, I need to come clean about some things, and all I ask is that you listen to what I have to say before saying anything in response, okay?"

Biting my lip, bracing myself for the words, "Gee, I'm sorry Renee, but things are too complicated with you and I need to move on," I took a sip of water and nodded.

"God, it's so hard to look at those bruises and not just lose my mind."

"Not the first time I've had them. They'll disappear soon," I whispered.

Cliff sighed. "I know. And I'm so very sorry you've...experienced such pain. Makes me glad Billy is behind concrete walls. If he ever gets paroled and has the balls to come back to Whitten County, I'll make sure he pays for every time he hit you."

"That's what you wanted to tell me?"

"No. I just...I love you and seeing you hurt, no matter what the cause, kills me. No, it makes me want to kill someone."

Unsure what to say, I stuffed a huge chunk of bread in my mouth. He just said he loved me, and part of me wanted to jump up on the table and shout out to the entire world, "This wonderful man is in love with me!" and the other part wanted to cry because I dreaded what was coming next.

"Okay, I've danced around this enough. I didn't just come back for you. I came back to Ridgeport because I was asked to."

Wow, that was completely out of left field. "Come again?"

"Remember Traci said Mayor Cayhill hired a private investigator when Martha disappeared?"

"Yes," I answered, my stomach quivering.

"He suspected something was wrong, especially after Mayor Cayhill let it slip about the land deal. Instead of investigating, he took what he'd uncovered, and went to Jared. The State Police opened a sting operation. Jared called me when I was still in Texas. He knew I was from Ridgeport and thought I could help. They figured I'd have no problem getting hired on at the Sheriff's Office considering my background and they were right. So, between me and the undercover cops posing as lawyers, we've been gathering evidence to nail Petyon. Cayhill's been meeting with them instead of the real deal all this time. That's why we all showed up at Traci's in time."

It took a few seconds to process that. "Wait, are you saying you've known—been involved—all this time? You were just using me to solve a crime?"

Cliff's face fell. "I knew something was wrong all this time, yes. But no, I wasn't using you! I didn't know how you tied into all this until the night you found the picture."

A hint of anger bubbled in my chest. "But you didn't come back to start things up with me, did you?"

231

Cliff d ropped h is e yes t o t he p late of bread. "No. But I swear Renee, the minute I saw you, I remembered how much you meant to me. Why do you think I started following you? I told you already I was trying to figure out a way to approach you. And what I said is the God's honest truth about the night I followed you to Bradford Lake. My gut instincts never lie to me. But, when I realized you were in danger, and after being around you again, it dawned on me how much I really did love you."

I wanted to be angry with him, but I couldn't. Everyone had secrets—things locked inside their hearts—they didn't want others to discover. I had my own I was keeping from him, and would never reveal. At least he was being honest with me. Coming clean took a lot of courage.

This time, I reached out for his hand. A shimmer of tears glinted behind his eyes when I did. "You know what Cliff? Sometimes circumstances just work out where good things happen in the midst of bad situations. You're here; I'm here,

232

regardless of how it happened. Let's just go chalk it up to fate and her twisted ways, and move forward. Okay?"

"Like I said before, love, wherever you go, I'm right next to you. I meant it then and I mean it now."

Smiling through my own tears, I gave Cliff's hand a final squeeze, letting go when the waiter brought our dinner.

We spent the next two hours discussing the craziness in Whitten County, bypassing our personal feelings toward each other. Cliff asked about my visit with the doctor and I cringed. Instead of lying to him like I did to Eleanor, I told him the truth. He insisted I contact the surgeons and set up appointments.

I countered with the fact I had no insurance and probably no job after what had happened. A big, easy smile graced his face when he told me not to worry about such trivial things, saying he'd make sure, if I truly needed surgery, it would happen. I didn't want to think about it so I changed the subject.

We came to the conclusion Mayor Cayhill either hired me to keep me under observation, assuming I knew the truth about Martha and hoping the offer of money and the bribe to keep Billy in jail would keep my mouth shut about the night at the lake, or to forever keep me in his debt should I figure things out if I didn't already know.

We also concluded the picture dropped off a t E leanor's w as p robably d one by someone hired by the Mayor to push me into revealing what I knew about the night. It tied in perfectly to Traci's attempts to weasel information from me about what I remembered about my father. Both Cliff and I reasoned Cayhill figured my mother might have told me she murdered Cyndi and Dad at the lake and maybe saw Martha slink away.

"You know, I still don't understand why Traci was involved, or why they picked poor Kendrick Paulson as the fall guy."

Cliff wiped a smear of garlic sauce from his chin and smiled. "Traci's aunt Sylvia deeded all the land over to Traci last year. If the manufacturing plant went through, part of the deal meant several acres around the entire lake would be converted to commercial rather than residential. Kendrick was an easy mark. Old, sick, and a loner. Singleton actually took some of Kendrick's blood to the doctor so test results would return as positive for cancer if anyone ever checked."

"Oh, my God, are you serious? Did he really think that'd work?"

"Seems so. People don't usually question such a harsh diagnosis. They just feel sorry for you and thank their lucky stars they aren't the one struck down by such a horrible disease. He might have gotten away with it, at least until the deal went through, then had some sort of miraculous recovery. Who knows what he was thinking? We'll learn more after he starts talking, which I guarantee you he will. He'll want to cut a deal, you watch. In terms of Traci's reason for getting involved, it was purely from greed."

"You think Traci assumed the land would sell for a lot of money then?"

"I don't think, I know. She called one of

the fake attorneys after a one of the meetings with Cayhill several months ago. She asked if they'd be interested in buying twenty acres. When they said yes and quoted her some outrageous figure, s he a pparently c ame on board."

"That bitch," I muttered. "And I thought Gretchen was bad."

"The phrase I heard was Traci the Twat. When we were flying down Highway 9 and I heard that, I laughed out loud. Some mouth you've got on you, girl."

I took a bite of pasta, enjoying the look of amusement on Cliff's f ace. " You know, Deputy, if you hurry up and eat, I'll show you what else my mouth can do."

I'd never seen anybody eat so fast in my entire life.

ELEANOR CALLED ON our way back to Ridgeport, informing us the reporters had migrated from her front yard over to Judge Singleton's place, and that it was safe to come home.

After hanging up I laughed. "Eleanor's sort of enjoying all the hustle and bustle I think."

"Can you blame her? The biggest scandal to hit Whitten County in, oh, pretty much ever, and her favorite gal's smack dab in the middle of it."

"I don't think her interest is just because of me. I can't remember if I told you or not, but she's kind of close to Kendrick. She mentioned she'd go out once a month to check on him, bring him food and such, you know, just to make sure he knew someone cared? It really bothered her when he got arrested. At least he'll be able to go home now and live his remaining days in peace."

After getting tossed and smacked around the day before, plus sitting in an interrogation room for hours, my back was thumping. I shifted in the seat several times trying to find a comfortable spot.

Cliff noticed and asked, "It's really bad, isn't it?"

Grimacing, I nodded. "Yes. Advanced osteoarthritis. Dr. Crusher said I needed to have two discs fused together. But, the pain will subside now that I'm not in danger of being knocked unconscious again."

"Bullshit. Well, I mean bullshit about the pain easing up, not about the other thing. No one will ever hurt you again, Renee. That's a promise. You got those numbers of the two surgeons with you?"

"I think so, why?"

"Call them both, right now, and get appointments scheduled."

"Cliff, we talked about this earlier. I don't have insurance or—"

"Renee, stop. I have plenty of money. Well, I'm not a millionaire or anything like that, but I've been frugal with my income over the years. Never married, no kids, and lived in military housing. I'm paying for the surgery and that's final."

"I can't let you do that. I mean I

appreciate the offer, but there are other things to consider, too."

"Such as?"

"For starters, I don't want to have the surgery. Second, someone will need to take care of me for a while after, and I'm not putting that burden on Eleanor or you. Third, even if I did have the surgery, then what? I'm back at the beginning of this nightmare with no job and a house to pay for. I've got to concentrate on finding work, first. If I snag a job with insurance benefits, I'd feel better about things. Surgery can wait until I get my life back in order."

"Renee, stop. You need the surgery. Now. You won't last six months at a job in the condition your back's in, I can see it in your face. I didn't buy my place, I'm just renting. I'll simply give my thirty-days' notice, move in with you, and take care of you while you recover. Well, I certainly will try to get some time in. I'm sure Eleanor will hover over you like a Momma hen."

The look of sheer determination to woo me to see his point of view made me smile.

"You've got it all figured o ut, d on't you Deputy?"

Cliff grinned. "Not all of it, but certainly most. The rest we'll just wing. Now, call Eleanor and tell her you're staying with me tonight. I plan on pampering you."

Shaking my head, overwhelmed with Cliff's g enerosity a nd l ove, I p unched in Eleanor's number. When I told her my plan, she laughed and said she'd figured as much.

The woman didn't miss a thing.

"THIS HOT TUB is amazing! Forget back surgery. I'll just sell my house and move in here."

"That's why I rented this place. It certainly wasn't for the spacious closets," Cliff yelled from the kitchen.

The two-bedroom house was small, situated on a small hill overlooking downtown Ridgeport. I'd driven by it before

240

numerous times and never imagined it was so nice inside because the exterior looked like all the others around town. Boring, bland, with no fancy landscaping or hint of the attention to detail inside.

The bathroom was big enough to hold a separate shower, dual sinks, and a hot tub with six seats. I'd gasped in shock when I first stepped inside. In my entire life, I'd never soaked in one, and the experience was amazing.

Once again, I'd given up on life *way* too soon.

The jets of hot water were magical. Though not completely gone, the throbbing in my lower back was tolerable. I looked at my fingers and laughed. They were so crinkled I looked like I was over one-hundred.

"Dinner's ready if you're done playing in the water," Cliff called from the hallway. "Want some help getting out?"

"Uh, no, I'm good. Be right there," I answered back.

The lights in the bathroom were bright,

and I wasn't ready to reveal all my faults to Cliff j ust y et. T he s exual h eat b etween us both was high tonight, and I knew what we'd end up doing before midnight rolled around. On one hand, I was eager and ready, but the other hand screamed for me to wait until in a dark room.

"Damn, you just keep shooting me down. My plan to seduce you so far is a failure," Cliff laughed.

I waited until I heard him walk away then eased out of the tub. There was a bottle of baby oil under the sink so I oiled my water-logged skin up. Looking down at the pile of clothes I had on earlier, I groaned. They weren't exactly fresh. With my makeup all gone, hair a damp mess, wrinkled clothes and dark bruises, I'd make a fine specimen.

In the mirror, I noticed a robe hanging on the door. Yanking it off, I tried it on. Though a bit long in the arms, the material was soft and warm and smelled of fresh linen. "Okay, here I go. I know what's going to happen next. Let it. Push away the old fears. Cliff isn't Billy. He'll be tender and loving. Gentle. Not all men are monsters."

My palms were sweating already. I wiped them on a towel and opened the door. The smells of dinner filled the hallway, along with a trail of white and red rose petals on the floor leading to the kitchen. Several votive candles were placed along the way, their gentle flickers guiding me toward my destination in the dark house. The sounds of light jazz rang through the rooms.

Rounding the corner, I stopped in the doorway to the small dining area. Just like at Eleanor's, dinner sat ready on the table with additional candles interspersed between the plates. Unlike Eleanor's the plates were paper and the cups red plastic.

Cliff stood next to a chair, a seductive grin on his face. He'd changed clothes and wore a loose pair of sleep pants and a thin, cotton t-shirt. Muscles bulged underneath the material as he pulled out the chair. "Madam, dinner is served. Love the robe."

I laughed as I walked over and sat. "Hamburgers and French fries? Perfect choices! I'm just a simple country gal so this is spot on."

"You're anything but simple, Renee. Strong. Complicated. A fighter, and the only person I've ever considered sharing my bed permanently with."

"That was smooth, Deputy. You're doing just fine w ith t he w hole seduction-thing. Promise."

"Good to hear! Now, eat, because what I have planned for us next will require energy."

I took a bite of the hamburger, surprised it was really good. "What did you put in here?"

"Oh, I can't share all my secrets with you. Must leave some things to the imagination."

I laughed and dug in, enjoying the food and company. My stomach was in knots, knowing what was coming next.

"What's wrong? Did I under cook it or something?"

"No, it's fabulous. Really. I'm just...uh, I don't know how to say this and not sound pathetic."

Cliff reached across the table and took my hand. "Nothing you say is ever pathetic. I'm listening."

Heat rolled up from my chest. "Okay, here goes. I haven't been...intimate with anyone in a very long time. A *very* long time. I'm nervous I won't live up to your expectations."

With gentle urging, Cliff stood and pulled me to him. I thought he was going to kiss me but instead, we swayed to the music, moving in small shuffles around the room. "Renee, the only expectation I have is to make you scream out my name. I've waited over thirty years to make you cum."

I almost did right then. My worries about being as dry as the Sahara were a waste, because I was practically dripping wet. "Then make me," I whispered, my voice husky with passion.

Cliff's reaction was immediate. Scooping me into his arms, he carried me down the hall to the bedroom. The comforter was pulled back already, revealing more rose petals on the sheets. He eased me down, his lips never breaking their hungry kiss on my own.

Shaking from desire and worry, I held still while he untied the robe. His mouth moved down my neck and chest, leaving a trail of wetness and heat until he found my nipple. When he took it into his mouth, I groaned with delight as his hot tongue licked and caressed.

"You're more beautiful than what I dreamed," he mumbled into my breast. "Let's see if you taste as sweet as them, too."

Cliff yanked off his shirt and pants and I groaned again as his flesh connected with mine. When his strong fingers entered me, I gasped. His lips found mine and he brought me to an orgasm in seconds.

"I didn't hear my name, so my job's not finished yet."

I'd never experienced so much raw passion. My hands couldn't touch his body fast enough. Bucking my hips, I welcomed all of him inside me. We rocked in heated harmony, his strokes deep and strong.

Mind-numbing bliss overrode everything

else. The pleasure was beyond anything I'd ever imagined. The intensity built to a crescendo as I sunk my fingers into Cliff's strong butt muscles, shoving him deeper inside me.

"Oh, God, Cliff! Oh, God! Fuck me!" I screamed as wave after wave of bliss exploded out of me.

And fuck me he did. Cliff's head dipped down and he found my nipple again, sucking hard as he rode his own orgasm. "All mine, Renee!" he groaned, followed by heavy grunts as he came.

Rather than pull out, Cliff wrapped his arms around me and we rolled over until we were facing each other. Both of us were covered in sweat, breathing hard.

"That was...amazing."

"Beyond," I whispered.

"I'm not moving my cock. Ever. It's home now," Cliff chuckled.

I gave it a little squeeze with my vaginal muscles, which apparently, still worked. "Wrong. I believe I still need to demonstrate what my mouth can do."

Cliff's hand reached up and wiped a lock of damp hair from my face. "You're going to have to wait a few minutes. I'm not a spring chicken, you know."

Nuzzling my head against his chest, inhaling his delicious scent, I responded, "I've waited my whole life to feel like this. What's another few minutes?"

AFTER THE NIGHT spent in sexual bliss with Cliff, things in my life finally took a turn for the better. Oh, hell, who was I kidding? Life did a one-eighty. Sometimes, while I slept curled up against Cliff, and listened to him breathe, I wondered if I'd stepped into an alternate reality because I was in Heaven.

For a few months, things in Ridgeport were insane. At the urging of Eleanor and Cliff, I finally gave an interview to a reporter.

On my terms, not his. Cliff set it up, had the guy come with only one cameraman to his house, and for thirty minutes, I told my side of the story.

Well, not all of it. I did leave out one particular detail.

Suddenly, I was a quasi-celebrity. Gretchen had the balls to call me and ask if I'd like to get together and "Hash things out," over dinner. I told her to go fuck herself and hung up. Myrtle from City Hall called about a week after the news broke and asked me if I wanted to come back to work. I told her to fuck off, too.

Kendrick Paulson, J r, died one week after being released from jail, Eleanor by his side when he passed. She'd tried to convince the man to come stay with her, but he was adamant about returning home. So, Eleanor went to visit him every day, cooking, cleaning, and caring for his needs. The last day he was alive, he gave Eleanor a small metal box and told her not to open it until he died.

No one attended his funeral except the three of us.

After leaving the graveside service, we took Eleanor home. She asked us to stay while she opened the box. Inside was a handwritten Last Will and Testament of Kendrick Paulson, Jr., written and notarized ten years prior. It left all he had, including the house and five acres it sat on, to Eleanor.

She cried and so did I.

The state dredged Bradford Lake for two days after the arrests of Cayhill and the others. They found the skeleton of Greenwood's wife the first day, chains full of algae and mud still wrapped around her arms and legs. After the discovery, plus their own damning words I'd recorded, the former mayor and detective both pleaded guilty and were sentenced to life down in Varner.

The second day of the dredging, my father's bike was discovered. The clothes I'd tied to it were gone, eaten away by the rancid water over time. When Cliff came home from work and told me, I cried. The tears were a mixture of sadness and shame, yet also tinged with relief.

Dad and Cyndi's remains were never found.

The manufacturing plant never was built, and Bradford Lake was officially closed. The natural spring that fed it was diverted by the state and plans to drain it were underway. There was some squabbling between the state entities about which one was responsible, which was rather comical. Why did it even matter?

The murky water remained, the area cordoned off by a ten-foot metal fence and the road blocked by a gate. Cliff said the gate had been repaired numerous times, probably from thrill seekers or nosy kids.

Traci's sentence was five years probation. The last I heard, she was still living in Sylvia's rental cabin and working part-time at Walmart over in the adjoining county.

Several Quorum Court members came over one night, begging Cliff to run for County Judge. I would have slammed the door in their face, but Cliff simply smiled, thanked them for the offer, and respectfully declined. A new mayor and judge were finally appointed, and each tried to wipe away the dark stains left by their predecessors. It was an uphill battle they'd yet to win.

"WHAT DID YOU say, sweetie? You're mumbling."

My eyelids were so heavy I struggled to open them. "Eleanor?"

"Of course, honey. Cliff had to use the restroom, so I'm pinch-hitting until he comes back."

"Wow, some meds they gave me. Is it over yet?"

Eleanor laughed. "No. You're still in pre-op."

"Oh. Silly me. No wonder I was thinking about so much in my head."

Leaning closer, Eleanor whispered, "You mentioned the lake several times."

"Did I? Damn. Hope I didn't say something I'll regret later," I muttered.

"No one would pay any attention. Don't worry. Ramblings of drugged patients are generally ignored."

Through the funk of medicine in my head, a question I'd wanted to ask Eleanor for months but didn't for fear of what she'd say, popped out. "You always knew about Martha, didn't you?"

Chuckling softly, Eleanor patted my hand. "Kendrick needed someone to talk to, and that person was me. He didn't become a hermit only because of what his daddy did. He feared Peyton just like everyone in Ridgeport did."

"Why?"

"Because Martha showed up at his house that night, cold, wet, covered in scratches and crying. She begged him to never tell anyone and he didn't. At least, not until he told me."

My eyelids lost the battle to remain open.

I felt myself slipping. "I'll be damned," I mumbled. Something else Eleanor said made me shiver. "You said everyone. Even you?"

"Yes, even me. Peyton feared I might know something, and he used it against me. Told me if I ever said a word, he'd make sure Billy served his entire sentence."

"Jesus, what an asshole. Ha, maybe they'll be cellmates."

"Doubtful. Billy made parole. He's coming home next week."

"Then it's a good thing we're moving back to Texas after I recover. Sorry, Eleanor, but you'll have to come visit me after I'm gone. I'm sure you understand why," I whispered then succumbed to the blackness.

"THE RING IS beautiful! Congratulations!" Eleanor gushed.

"Thank you," I said, holding my hand up so the diamond caught the light from the ceiling fan. "Cliff is always full of surprises. He put it on my breakfast tray this morning, nestled inside the napkin with the words "Will you?" written on it. So sweet. God, I can't believe it!"

"I'm so happy for you, Renee. Have you given thought about when and where?"

"Not really. I mean, I need to be able to walk down the aisle without limping first. The only thing I do know for sure is it won't happen here. Cliff suggested San Antonio, so once we get settled in his place, we'll figure it out."

"Am I invited?"

"Why wouldn't you be? You're like my second mom now," I said, pushing myself from the bed. "Someone's got to give me away."

Eleanor moved to help me but I shook my head, determined to do it myself.

"How far is San Antonio from here?"

"About seven hours. Don't worry, we already thought about that. Whatever spot we pick, we'll fly you in so you don't have to drive."

"Thank you, sweetie. So, how's the pain level today?"

"Not too bad, actually. Cliff went to the store to get more boxes. I know he won't let me help pack while he's here, so when he goes to work tonight, I'm going to surprise him. Get everything all labeled and stowed away. He's been working hard taking care of me plus actually working."

"Still leaving Saturday?" Eleanor asked.

"That's the plan. Signed the sale papers yesterday for my house, so there's nothing left to do but finish up here."

Eleanor followed behind me as I took tentative steps around the room. "Don't overdo it, Renee. Take smaller steps."

"I'm fine, Eleanor. Really. The incision hurts more than the fusion. Doc said by next week, I'll feel like a new woman."

"I heard the department threw Cliff a nice going away bash yesterday."

"They did. The new Sheriff tried to talk him into staying on. Even offered him Greenwood's old job. I thought it was funny.

After all that's happened, why would the man even consider Cliff would stay?"

"Some people just don't like to say goodbye. Especially to those they love."

Hearing the hitch in Eleanor's voice, I turned around. Sure enough, she was crying. "This isn't goodbye, Eleanor. It's see you later. Texas isn't in another country you know."

"I know," Eleanor said, wiping the tears away. "I'm just really going to miss you."

"I'll miss you too, but we'll stay in touch. You are welcome to come visit anytime. At least you aren't alone now that Billy's back home."

I really struggled to say the last part without sounding angry. Yes, my lovely ex was back in town. Joy. So far I'd been lucky, holed up at Cliff's, so I hadn't run into him. Cliff did at Walmart yesterday, and the two men nearly came to blows until several shoppers stepped in and separated them.

God, I couldn't *wait* to get out of this town.

"Speaking of, I need to go to the store

and pick up some more groceries. Billy sure does seem to enjoy my cooking."

Anything was better than prison food. I hoped the bastard would choke to death on a chicken bone or something. "Everyone enjoys your cooking, Eleanor. When I'm back up to par, I plan on making a huge pot of spaghetti—if you'll share your marinara recipe with me?"

Eleanor hugged me and walked to the door. She stopped and pulled out a piece of paper from her purse and set it on the dresser. "I know it's your favorite so I already wrote it down."

She didn't wait for me to say anything.

Once I heard Eleanor shut the front door, I walked over to the dresser and picked up the paper. In her beautiful handwriting, Eleanor had written out the recipe, dated it, and signed it. *With all my love to a woman stronger than me—Mom #2.*

Smiling, I headed to the bathroom to take a shower, grateful for many things, including the cherished bond between me and Eleanor. Three months ago, I was ready to kill myself.

Now, the horrible nightmares were gone, kept at bay each night by Cliff's strong arms, and I was days away from leaving my wretched life behind in Arkansas to begin a new one in Texas.

With my future husband.

"God, thank you!" I whispered while staring at the diamond on my finger. "Thank you."

"YOU NEED HELP getting out?"

"It feels so good I think I'll stay in it a few more minutes."

"No way. You might slip and fall. Come on, future wife, let me help."

"Okay, okay. Worry wort," I muttered. Cliff helped me out of the hot tub and back to the bed.

"Stay put, Renee. I mean it. I saw how you looked at those boxes earlier. If just one of them is packed when I get off duty, I'll put you over my knee."

My response was a coy grin. "That sounds like fun and not a deterrent."

Cliff returned the grin. "Just wait until you get better. I'm going to make you scream so loud the neighbors will think I'm killing you."

"Oh, can't wait! Now go. I promise I won't stuff one item in a box. Quit worrying."

Cliff kissed my forehead then adjusted his holster. "Got your phone?"

"Right here," I replied, holding it up. "You've been hanging out with Eleanor too much. Her fretting rubbed off on you."

"Hey, people are supposed to fret over those they love, remember? I'll stop by on my break to check on you. Love you, Renee. Get some rest."

"Love you, too, babe. Enjoy your last day! Oh, tomorrow we start the day off both unemployed!"

Cliff laughed while tromping down the hall. I waited a full fifteen minutes after he left before slinking back out of bed and back to the bathroom. The hot tub was addicting, and I preferred to soak in the bubbly water rather than take pain medication. Another ten or fifteen minutes of the jets massaging my back and I'd sleep like a baby.

I sure would miss the hot tub when we moved. Maybe Cliff would be willing to—

"Crap! I knew he'd come back and catch me!"

Struggling to get out without falling, I scrambled out of the tub and flung my robe on. I could hear Cliff's boots coming down the hall. Jesus, I wish I could move faster and hop back in bed! He was going to be mad at me if he knew I'd risked getting into the slippery tub alone.

I made it to the bed then remembered I left my cell on the bathroom counter. Damnit! Oh well, if Cliff noticed and asked, I'd tell him I forgot to bring it back to bed after using the restroom.

"Hello, darling. Miss me?"

The sound of Billy's deep, menacing voice made my skin quiver and heart pound.

My hands shook and legs trembled as old fears seized my soul.

"If Cliff catches you, he'll—"

Billy stepped through the doorway, the evil smirk he always wore beaming. "He won't catch me because I'll only be here a minute. Maybe two."

"Get out," I hissed.

Crossing the room in three long strides, Billy's strong fingers dug into my forearm. "My thoughts exactly. Let's get out of here. We've got places to go and people to see."

"I'm not going anywhere with you," I said but not with enough conviction.

Billy's breath was rank, full of the scent of bourbon and cigarettes. The stench took me back years. Those hateful eyes I used to have nightmares about stared back at me, red and swollen. He hadn't aged well in prison. He looked old, scraggly, and pissed as hell. I'd seen the look so many times I knew what was coming next.

Billy jerked me toward the door and I yelped in pain. "Where's your phone?"

"Screw...you," I mumbled through

clenched teeth. "I'm not afraid of you anymore, Billy Runsford."

He yanked me closer so my face was millimeters from his own. "You should be. Tell me where it is and I might consider letting you live."

"No."

I knew it was coming and I didn't care. I wouldn't cower down to him again. The back of Billy's hand caught my cheek. He didn't hit me hard enough to knock me down, only enough to ring my bell. "Got mouthy while I was away, huh? I'll fix that. I surely will. I've waited for this for a very, very long time."

I spit the mouthful of blood in his face, which turned out to be a mistake.

"WAKE UP YOU little Jezebel. You've got a phone call to make."

It took me a second to open my eyes. When I did, I realized I was in a truck, it was dark outside, and I was freezing. Licking my lips, I tasted the rusty flavor of blood. My head and back throbbed, as well as my swollen lip. I felt something warm and squishy underneath my arm.

Crumbled in the seat next to me was Eleanor. A large gash starting from her scalp and down past her cheek gushed blood all over the front of her shirt.

Stifling a gasp, I sat up, tears rolling down my face.

Billy tossed my cell into my lap. "Call him."

My heart sank. "No. Whatever you got planned is between the two of us. Leave him and Eleanor out of it this. She's your mother, Billy! She loves you—"

"Shut up!" Billy roared. "I said call him. If you don't, when he arrives, I'll kill both of them real slow and make you watch. I swear I will Renee."

I knew my ex well enough to know he meant every word. Fumbling with the phone, praying silently Eleanor would wake up, or God Himself would swoop down and take hold of the wheel, my shaking hands dropped the phone.

"Quit stalling or I swear Renee—"

"Give me a minute, please Billy? I just had surgery," I begged while feeling around the floorboard. I felt something soft. Eleanor's purse! Digging further, I let my fingers search for something, anything I could use as a weapon. My heart skipped two beats when I realized there was nothing inside to help me. "Got it."

"Call him and put him on speaker. If you say one word, I'll slit her throat right here and let her bleed all over you. Understand?"

"Yes," I mumbled, softly crying as I hit send and called Cliff.

"Hey baby! Miss me already?"

I had to cover my mouth to contain my sobs when I heard Cliff's sweet voice.

"You'll be missing her forever if you don't follow exactly what I'm about to say, Cliffie-Boy," Billy said, his tone dark and almost playful. "You ready to play a fun game?"

There was a long pause before Cliff

answered. I prayed the call dropped but again, I didn't have that kind of luck. "If you hurt her Runsford, I promise you'll regret it."

"Big talk for a man who's soon to be wife is sitting next to me, bleeding. You're trying my patience, Cliffie-Boy. Ready for the rules?"

"Yes," Cliff responded in a hushed, angry tone.

"Good. There are only three, so here goes. Come alone; tell a soul and their dead; and hurry, you've got fifteen minutes or both of them will be taking a permanent swim. I assume you're smart enough to figure out where."

Billy rolled down the window and tossed my phone out as we sped down Highway 9 toward Suicide Lake.

God, help us.

Please?

15

THE GATE WAS busted—again—when
Billy turned down the dirt highway leading
to the lake. Rumbles of thunder in the
distance made the truck vibrate with each
boom. The storm was close and it would be
a wicked one judging by the thick bolts of
lightning. Dainty white snowflakes peppered
the windshield. Ignoring the freak
thundersnow storm, I zoned in on just one

thing I remembered Billy probably didn't count on.

Billy didn't know how to swim.

Bouncing down a dark road, I stared ahead, refusing to look at the piece of shit behind the wheel. He knew I was terrified and I wouldn't give him the satisfaction of seeing it on my face while I figured out how I was going to get him near the water and push his sorry ass in. I'd probably end up going in with him, but I didn't care. If it meant I'd save Cliff and Eleanor, at least my death at Suicide Lake would be a valiant one.

"Your mother loves you, Billy. She went every month to see you, stood by your side at the trial, never gave up on you, and this is how you repay her?"

"No one betrays me and gets away with it. No one. Just ask my dead second wife," Billy said then threw the truck in park. "Guess I didn't train you well enough to remember, huh? Now, get out and walk to the hood. Move one step more and it will be your last."

Opening the door, I stepped out into the cold night air. The robe was thick, but not thick enough. The cold made me shiver even harder, which aggravated my back. It took all the strength I had to push through the pain and walk.

Billy groaned as he lugged Eleanor's unconscious body from the front seat of the truck. The movement made his jacket flop open. The shakes intensified when I saw the butt of some sort of pistol sticking up from his waist. Squatting to get better traction, he hefted once and slung Eleanor over his shoulder.

"Go to the end of the dock. Slow," Billy instructed. For emphasis, he pulled the gun from his beltline and pointed it at Eleanor's back. "No tricks or she'll pay the price."

The deck was slippery and I was barefooted. My teeth were chattering by the time I made it to the end. Billy was breathing hard while trudging behind me. Just as I turned around, he dropped Eleanor's body onto the wood. Eleanor groaned yet didn't move. Billy turned to me and smiled. The look on his face was horrifying.

"You shouldn't have disobeyed me,

Renee. You belong to me, remember? No man was to ever touch you again. It was part of your punishment for what you did. I forgave you for taking back your old name but marrying another is unforgivable."

"All these years and you still blame me for William's death? I was a good Mom, Billy. William died because of sudden infant death—"

"Liar!" Billy roared, grabbing my wrist and twisting hard. "He died because of your sins! I left you because I couldn't stand being near you any longer. That was my sin. I gave up because I was weak. Now, I'm not. William died because God took him for your sins! That's why you had to pay. Why I had to make you pay. I couldn't just let you get away with it!"

Fighting back the tears, I stared into his eyes. I needed to figure out what he meant and how I could use the situation to throw him off balance mentally, then follow it up by physically. "Pay for what, Billy? Sleeping with you before we got married?"

"Devil's mouth. You've always had a

devil's mouth, Renee. He's the father of lies and you are his daughter. That's why you're here, along with my traitorous mother and soon, the other you fornicated with and duped into marriage."

"Billy, please, whatever you're thinking, leave them out of it. Again, this is just between the two of us."

"Wrong! You need to pay for what you did. You were doing a good job all those years you were alone. I know because I had others keep an eye on you. But then you wormed your way inside Mom's head with your lies. Now you're about to ruin another man's life because you can't tell the truth, so I won't let you."

Frustrated, I blurted out, "Tell the truth about what, Billy?"

Pulling me to him, Billy stroked my cheek with the tip of the cold steel. "That you're a killer."

My mind gridlocked.

The strokes to my cheek increased in pressure to match Billy's words. "Your penance for your sins are two-fold. First, you'll find s weet f reedom b y c oming clean and telling my good ol' mommy and your betrothed who really killed your dad and his whore. Second, I'm going to kill both of them—right in front of your eyes—and let you take the fall for it. You'll get to spend the remainder of your life behind bars paying for your mistakes like I did. It's only fair, Renee. I killed and took my punishment. Now it's time for you to do the same."

"How did you...I never told you!" I yelled, shocked by the revelation.

"Those pills that brain doc gave you years ago. They made you talk in your sleep. Of course, I didn't believe it at first but you kept having the same dream. Waking me up in the middle of the night, crying and yelling about your daddy. So, I came here and did a little diving. Imagine my surprise when I found their bones and the bike, just like you said in the dream, right about six feet from this here dock. I was young and stupid, still sort of in love with you but you committed murder! Instead of turning you in, I got all the bones I could find a nd b rought them home. Remember the night we roasted a pig?"

"Oh, God, you didn't—?"

"I did. Had to get the coals hot enough to turn the bones from your sins into ashes. As your husband, it was my job to make you pay for committing murder. You were a good girl, taking your punishment and even stayed all these years after I left. A miserable life was your sentence so I'm afraid a good one just isn't in the cards for you."

The fight in me was gone, replaced by utter shock and confusion. Billy's words opened up my mind to the truth. I did stay, at least subconsciously, in Ridgeport to atone for what I did as a teenager. I shoved my own feet into the mud and mentally tethered myself to the town.

A large piece of my soul died on the edge of the dock.

In the distance, I heard the crunch of tires but couldn't move.

"Oh, don't look so sad, baby. Sounds like lover boy arrived. Since it's so cold, let's warm each other up and give him a show before he dies. Kind of cold out here tonight. For old time's sake."

Billy slid the gun between my legs as he untied the robe. The other hand was cold as it crushed my breast. I closed my eyes, unwilling to look into his disturbed, demented face anymore.

I said a silent prayer for Eleanor, hoping Cliff would get her to a hospital in time. I followed it with another, asking God to comfort Cliff's heart, and a final one to ask for forgiveness for what I was about to do, which was kill again.

"Sink or swim, asshole!" I yelled while bringing my knee up with everything in me into Billy's crotch. He groaned and doubled over, one hand still firmly clutching the edge of the robe. He lost his balance and over we went.

Right before my head broke the surface of the water, I heard Eleanor and Cliff both scream.

The near-freezing liquid took my breath away. The water was dark and I couldn't see a thing, though I felt Billy's feet and fists flop about as he struggled to swim.

For a split second, I considered letting myself join my ex. The urge to let the water swallow me up like I wanted it to not long ago didn't last long. It was replaced by the will to live.

To help Eleanor.

To see Cliff's face again.

To not let Billy Runsford win.

To no longer suffer and pay for mistakes of my past.

Forcing my freezing limbs to work, I swam toward the surface. A streak of lightning helped guide me. When I didn't think my legs could kick anymore, something grabbed my arm and suddenly, I could breathe.

"Renee, oh my, God!" Cliff yelled while pulling me to him.

I couldn't have moved had I wanted to. I was shaking so hard I was having trouble breathing. Cliff eased me to the ground after my legs buckled.

"Eleanor? Where's Eleanor?" I asked.

"Right here, baby. Shh, hush now. Save your strength. Clifton, you best get on that radio and call for the cavalry then get us some blankets before this girl goes into hypothermia."

Cliff pulled his jacket off and covered my shoulders as Eleanor wrapped her arms around me. The dock shook as Cliff took off toward his car, screaming into his microphone while running.

"I'm so sorry, Renee. So very sorry," Eleanor cooed as she looked behind me and out over the water.

"Me, too," I whispered, knowing the pain she must be feeling for losing her child, and oddly surprised she hadn't jumped in to try and save him.

"Don't be. Billy deserved what happened. I didn't want to believe my son was a monster but tonight he proved me wrong. He flew into a rage when I confirmed y ou were getting remarried. At first, h e o nly t ore up the house but when he came after me, I...well, I now understand the terror you endured for so long. I tried to get to the phone and warn you but that's when he attacked me. I swear if I had any inkling he was planning any of this..." Eleanor's voice trailed off as she started to cry.

Still shaking, I forced myself to say, "I know, Eleanor. I know. I'm so sorry he hurt you."

"Ditto," Eleanor mumbled.

Looking up, I watched Cliff slam the trunk of his unit shut and head back our way. Before he made it back within hearing range, I asked, "Did you...hear everything?"

Eleanor looked at me, her eyes full of too many emotions to read. A few snowflakes floated down, landing on her wet cheeks and bloody gash. She nodded once and smiled while rubbing my back. "Some things are meant to stay hidden, Renee. I know how to keep secrets. Had plenty of practice over the years. I believe you've more than paid your penance for what happened out here so many years ago. You just let me do the talking when questions start flying, okay? I'll make sure this last secret stays at Suicide Lake."

Had I been able to do anything besides

shake, I would have cried and hugged her back. Instead, I hoped the look I gave Eleanor truly conveyed my thankfulness and love. It must have, because she gave me a final pat and said, "Your love is coming back. Take good care of him, Renee. He loves you so."

"I will," I finally managed.

Eleanor helped me stand when Cliff returned, blankets in hand. I collapsed into his arms, grateful they were still there to hold me.

And that Eleanor would make sure they always would be.

"Oh, baby, I'm so sorry. It's my fault! I shouldn't have left you alone." Cliff whispered in my ear while hugging me tight.

Sirens wailed in the distance as I shook in Cliff's arms. "None of this had anything to do with you, Cliff. Don't even go there."

"Renee's right, Cliff. Put the blame where it belongs, which is on my son's shoulders," Eleanor added.

"Damn, I lost my ring in the water," I muttered. For some reason, the loss overwhelmed me and I started to cry. The lake owned too many pieces of my life.

"Doesn't matter. I'll get you a new one. The most important thing in my world is still here," Cliff cooed. "And I always will be."

I pulled away and looked at Cliff and knew he meant every word. "Me, too. I love you, Cliff Simpson."

"Enough mushy crap. Cliff, get her into your car where it's warm until the ambulance gets here. You two have a lifetime to fawn over each other."

"On it," Cliff said. He picked me up and carried me down the dock.

With one last look over Cliff's shoulder, I mentally cursed the lake, thankful I'd never have to see it again. And I vowed to not let its secrets haunt the rest of my life. My new life as Mrs. Cliff Simpson.

ABOUT THE AUTHOR

Award-winning and International bestselling author Ashley Fontainne is an avid reader of mostly the classics. Ashley became a fan of the written word in her youth, starting with the Nancy Drew mystery series. Stories that immerse the reader deep into the human psyche and the monsters lurking within us are her favorite reads.

Her muse for penning the *Eviscerating the Snake* series was *The Count of Monte Cristo* by Alexandre Dumas. Ashley's love for this book is what sparked her desire to write her debut novel, *Accountable to None*, the first book in the trilogy. With a modern setting to the tale, Ashley delves into just what lengths a person is willing to go to when they seeking personal justice for heinous acts perpetrated upon them. The second novel in the series, *Zero Balance.* focuses on the cost and reciprocal cycle that obtaining revenge has on the seeker. For once the cycle starts, where does it end? How far will the tendrils of revenge expand? *Adjusting Journal Entries* answered that question: far and wide.

Her short thriller entitled *Number Seventy-Five*, touches upon the sometimes dangerous world of online dating. *Number Seventy-Five* took home the BRONZE medal in fiction/suspense at the 2013 Readers' Favorite International Book Awards contest and is currently in production for a feature film.

Her paranormal thriller entitled *The Lie*, won the GOLD medal in the 2013 Illumination Book Awards for fiction/suspense and is also in production for a feature film entitled *Foreseen*.

Ashley's decided to delve into the paranormal with a Southern Gothic horror/suspense novel, *Growl*, which released in January of 2015. The suspenseful mystery *Empty Shell*, released in September of 2014. Ashley teamed up with Lillian Hansen (Ashley calls her mom!) and penned a three-part murder mystery/suspense series entitled *The Magnolia Series*. The first book, *Blood Ties*, released the Summer of 2015, and was voted one of the Top 50 Self-Published Books You Should Be Reading in 2015 at www.readfree.ly.

Whispered Pain released in October of 2015 and *Night Court* released December 13, 2015. Ashley also penned a new zombie/post-apocalyptic series of books scheduled to release in 2016.

Connect with Ashley:

Website: http://www.ashleyfontainne.com – Sign up for Ashley's newsletter and receive a free ebook!

Twitter: https://twitter.com/ashleyfontainne

Facebook: https://www.facebook.com/ashley.fontainne

Movie site: http://www.foreseenmovie.com